# Pilgrim Souls

Also by Rose Helen Mitchell and published by Ginninderra Press

*Siege of Contraries*
*Whispering Shadows*
*Across Time & Place* (Pocket Poets)
*James Joyce, Ulysses & Ireland* (Pocket Polemics)
*Pasha* (Pocket People)

# Rose Helen Mitchell

# Pilgrim Souls

This work is dedicated with love and gratitude
to my friend, my daughter: Anne Marie

and to her daughter, Courtney Elizabeth James.


To mothers and daughters the world over:
love one another.


*Pilgrim Souls*
ISBN 978 1 74027 740 2
Copyright © text Rose Helen Mitchell 2012
www.rosehelenmitchell.com.au
Portrait photography: Tania Gaylor (www.TaniaGaylor.com)

First published 2012
Reprinted 2017

**GINNINDERRA PRESS**
PO Box 3461 Port Adelaide 5015
www.ginninderrapress.com.au

**1**

## Adelaide, July 2008

My pilgrimage to Scotland started on a cold wet Adelaide day. Earlier that morning I stood in Centennial Park cemetery beside a simple memorial marking my parents' existence:

Eleanor Banfield 1947–2007
Peter Banfield 1944–1995

I placed a bunch of rosemary on top of the headstone, whispered 'Goodbye' and trudged back to my car. Fat drops of water bombarded the roof and bonnet then sluiced down the windscreen. The noise drowned out my sobs. The mist on the windows gave me a measure of privacy to punch a good measure of my grief onto the empty passenger seat.

My dad died suddenly of a heart attack when I was ten years old. One morning he left Mum and me at the breakfast table while he took off on his usual four-kilometre run along the beach front. The next time we saw him, he lay frozen stiff in the hospital morgue. Mum was hysterical for days then silent for a long, long time. I learned how to mourn then. But I had Mum, and she had me, to cling to. Eventually, we garnered strength from each other and I thought she'd be with me forever.

Now my quest, to the other side of the world, is to meet family I never knew I had until a few months ago.

Finally, when the rain and tears had stopped and the clouds parted, I moved off. A white hazy sun shimmered in the depths of little pools on the cemetery lawns and pathways, like discs of hope. Hope that I'd like my newly found relatives and that they would like me.

A final quick message to my cousin Claire winged its way through the ether. I'd have two weeks to spend in Scotland and should arrive at Glasgow on the seventh of July. Uni accommodation for my time in London had been arranged. Travel gear I'd bought snuggled neatly in my shiny red soft suitcase in the hallway. Check: Passport. Credit cards. Euros. Airline tickets. Face wipes. Something to read: Milton? Novel? Norton? – too fat. I settled on my dog-eared copy of *Paradise Lost* and the prize-winning quirky *I Dream of Magda* by local lad Stefan Laszcuszk.

At the airport, Augie gave me the tiniest jade Buddha in a velvet pouch and wished me a safe journey.

Joe pulled a small wet towel from his pocket. 'Look at this. I've cried all fuckin' night 'cos you're leaving.' He hugged me so tight, I thought I'd break.

'It's okay, Joe, I know you'll miss me,' I said to his back as he galumphed across to the exit.

Mardi stayed until I'd gone through the departure gate. 'See you in Dubrovnik,' she called as I joined a straggly line of travellers along the glass-framed corridor stretched high above the tarmac.

Smiling airline staff greeted me like a familiar friend and directed me to a window seat from where I watched airport staff load rain-soaked baggage into the plane's hold. Shortly after the lurch and drone of take-off, we'd left the rain clouds behind and the plane headed up and over the interior of Australia. I checked the movie schedule, fiddled with the radio stations, read the emergency landing information and flipped through *The Australian Way* magazine.

I wanted to see Mum sitting right beside me. I wanted to ask questions about Scotland. About her parents and brothers. I wanted to say how sometimes I'm frightened about the future.

# 2

Since she was diagnosed with cancer, Mum had kept a diary. I'd found it under her pillow the day she'd gone into hospital for the last time, and put it away with her jewellery and favourite shawls. At the last minute of packing I'd wrapped it in one of her scarves and put it in my flight bag with the McCrae's of Glenhill file. Now, with nothing else to do but watch white clouds, I decided to take a look at her last written words. I draped the scarf on my shoulders and let the sweet scent of her sweep over me. When I opened the book, an envelope fell onto my lap. A letter. Addressed to me.

My dear Anna,

My heart sinks to the pit of my stomach when I think that you will soon be alone. I know that life doesn't always work the way we want it to, and I know that you will miss me, but I believe that unplanned interruptions and difficulties are some of the greatest friends of the soul. I want you to know that bad things happened to me in the past. You know nothing of these. Keeping you ignorant was a choice I made long ago. Nevertheless, they have shaded your life. I have written some of it in this journal but there are other things that are too painful to write about.

You have a generous heart, Anna, and I know that you will judge me kindly.

Remember the words of your literary hero 'mistakes are the portals of discovery'.

It is the strangest thing to look back over my life seeing what I have done with it, and I wonder now what I look like to you. I am so very proud of your achievements and I thank you for sharing your adventure in learning with me. You have taught me many lessons – through you I have learned not to hate my mother. The following words say all that is in my heart. I found them in *Anam Cara* – the book you gave me last Christmas. Remember?

On the day when the weight deadens on
Your shoulders and
You stumble, may the
Clay dance to balance you

And when your eyes
freeze behind
the grey window
and the ghost of loss
gets into you,
may a flock of colours
indigo, red, green
and azure blue
come to awaken in you
a meadow of delight.

I read the last stanza over and over until I'd memorised it. I took the folder out and studied the family snapshots again and wondered what she'd meant about hating her mother? She'd never told me anything about that. I started to read.

**3**

## 27 February 2007

*The tests are conclusive. We can start therapy tomorrow. Cancer, they said. Aggressive. Lungs. Brain. Liver. They refused to tell me how long of this life I have left but I know it will only be weeks. A month or two at most. It feels different from when they took the lump from my breast. Back then the news was good.*

*I'm tortured by feelings of guilt. Anna? Alone? How can I steal some time from this disease and hold back the moment when I have to tell her that I will be dead before her next birthday? I won't see her Honours graduation.*

*Where do I find the phrases that will ease the instant? How will I be able to talk to her about a future without me? How will I be able to talk to her about my funeral? My funeral – how bizarre! The words whisper. They sway in my mind like shadows in a changing light.*

## 28 February 2007

*Memento Mori. Limited mortality. It punches and batters its way into every waking second. Could it be a cruel rumour?*

*I've heard that when some people are faced with death, colours become brighter, sounds clearer. Deep plunging sadness is all I know, as if I'm slurping muck from a murky pool of darkness.*

## 7 March 2007

*This morning I walked on the beach and let the fringe of the sea froth around my toes. I remembered times when Peter, Anna and I ran along that beach.*

*I thought I saw spectres of our life together dance along the sand in front of me. When I closed my eyes for a few seconds, imaginary bits of our summer dresses floated and flung themselves at the breeze. I could see our long skinny legs extended so much by the sun it looked like we were on stilts.*

*A cool wind whipped through my shirt making it billow behind me and cooled my head. I thought maybe if I breathed deeply I'd win more time.*

*I want more time.*

*I am not ready to die!*

*I've never considered that disease and thoughts of mortality entail loneliness and isolation. It's as if I have already died.*

*Anna? What shape will her life take now?*

*The beach brings memories of mornings when we'd gathered shells and dived for stones in the shallows. Evenings when we'd eaten pizzas on a blanket wrinkled and damp from our wet, tanned bodies. I loved those times of our life. Loved the innocence of it.*

*Being near the sea reminds me of the day I met Peter. My first sight of him is so clear in my mind that thinking about it now, brings back the smell of that other sea and the touch of a softer sun on my face. I remember every detail. The first smile he gave to me was like receiving a gift. I have remembered that smile and through the years I have lived without him, I have never seen anything vaguely resembling it on a stranger's face without feeling a stab of pain.*

*I wish I could believe the preachings of my childhood and that death will reunite me with Peter in a blissful eternity. It would be so lovely to fold myself around him now, the way it was in our marriage bed.*


## *10 March 2007*

*Today, I walked for a long time, thinking about the plans Anna and I had made for the end of her Honours year when I'd show her around Scotland. Oban. Kate's place. That enchanting, healing home. We'd go to Gourock. Sail across to Dunoon. Walk through the hills of Argyllshire where Peter had walked. Art galleries. Castles. Cathedrals.*

*It won't happen now. I hope she will make the journey. I'd like that. Sometimes now, when I need so much help, I feel that Anna is the mother and I am the child.*

Confusion. Who was Kate? Mum had never mentioned her. Was she (or is she) part of the McCrae family? What role did she play in my mother's life?

Back to the first entry. No mention of Kate. What was too painful to talk about?

I made a note to ask Claire about Kate.

## 19 March 2007

*What can I say to Anna? Start with Peter? No. Something she doesn't know about? Place? Yes. Place. The beginning. Think about it. Tomorrow.*

*My story. My place. The west coast of Scotland.*

## 20 March 2007

*In 1964 the village where my character was formed had two main streets bordered by white houses with black roofs and long windows. Vale Street and Bridge Street formed a cross at a point we called 'the oval'. A corner of this patch was where the local bookie waited for the dreamers in the community to place their bets. During my growing up years, this spot was where gossip filtered from the Black Bull pub and Galbraith's grocery store. Where facts became distorted, and reputations were moulded or dismantled by idle talk.*

*In summer, fields of corn and wheat as high as a seven- or eight-year-old child's head surrounded the village. Now, I can close my eyes and picture wayward children making paths through the crops in quests for hidden adventures or playing childish war games. I can see flattened patches where we sat and rubbed the heads of grain before blowing the chaff away and devouring the sweet, fresh kernels. I see too, the season's wild roses that edged fields of potatoes. When their season was over and the blossoms lay* composting, we picked their legacy of rose hips from the hedgerows and sold them for pocket money.

I remember roadsides trimmed with bushes of fat hairy gooseberries and purplish-black brambles that made feasts for Sunday walkers and jam for breakfast toast. Today, my dry palate longs for the taste of that fruit.

Writing this has become painful. Too painful. My mind is saying it's important but the memories hurt my heart.

## 26 March 2007

I will tell Anna tonight. I wish Peter were here to help me through this. (I feel selfish for wishing this – it would be agony for him.)

As if she'd heard me thinking about her, Anna rang just now to say she's running late and she'll be home in an hour. Reprieve.

## 27 March 2007

She knows. We cried – crushed by our misery. She wants me to talk about my life in Scotland. She wants to know every tiny detail about how, where and when Peter and I met. I've held so much back from Anna and I don't know if I want her to know some things about me.

**4**

I couldn't read any more and put the diary aside. The night she told me the cancer had come back, we'd cried for a long time. I'd thrown books at the wall. Mum tried to calm me down with soothing words. I remember feeling guilty because I should have been consoling her.

With that thought, my eyes drooped shut and I turned my face to the window. My shoulders wouldn't stop shaking. Holding tight to the ends of her scarf helped. The tears rolled at will down my face. I thought about the words I'd just read and wondered what had happened to Mum in that village she'd described so beautifully.

What had she held back from me? And why did she?

I must have fallen asleep because the next thing I knew, the woman sitting beside me nudged me and said, 'Sorry about disturbing you but we're about to be served a meal.'

I answered a quiet 'Thank you,' then spent a few minutes turning my head from side to side trying to get the kinks out of my neck and shoulders.

'Have you read this one?' she asked, showing me a copy of *Angela's Ashes*.

'No, but I've heard it's very good.'

'Sure is… Irish Catholics didn't have much of a life, according to McCourt.'

She (Carol) rattled on about the poverty and deprivation of the author's family then started in on her own history. By the time we parted company at Singapore, she'd told me her life story and that of her entire family. I'd no chance to read more of Mum's diary until I was on the plane for London, grateful to be next to a vacant seat.

I don't know what I expected to find in Scotland. Perhaps some things Mum hadn't told me about herself. Photos of her childhood. Friends she grew up with. Something that would bring her alive again. Undisturbed thoughts about the past months charged through my head like a spinning prism of places and faces.

**5**

## Adelaide, August 2007

Rain dripped from my hair and slicked down my face. Water ran from my jacket onto my jeans, now sticking to my calves like a second skin. Getting soaked, while trying to fit a bent key into a lock to open a stubborn door, gave me a focus for my rage. I kicked and punched the door as if it was responsible for my feelings of abandonment. Rattling my key in the lock and heaving my body weight against it, the door finally gave way.

For a few seconds I stood leaning against the door and wiping rain from my face. The hush of the house hit me like a sledgehammer. The silence needed voices to interrupt it. I felt defeated by the weight of grief and anger. The idea that she'd deserted me hit me smack in the solar plexus as if I'd lost the power of steering.

The worst thing about Mum dying was coming home to the cold emptiness of a house that used to ring with music. If Mum had unpleasant chores to do, like cleaning the bathroom and toilet, she'd put on a disc by the Scottish Fiddle Orchestra. And if she were in a singing mood she'd play the songs of Elvis or Frank Sinatra.

The next worst thing was missing the sound of her voice when I opened the front door. I missed the endless questions: who did I meet? What happened at uni today? Did I have a good lunch? She'd go on with her intrusive infuriating questions like forever. I'd either grunt one-syllable responses or sidle off to my room. Now, eight weeks from her funeral, I'd give anything to hear her ask them again.

I moved inside and the thump of my feet echoed off the walls as if someone was walking beside me. The noise of my backpack landing on the floor reverberated like the echo of a door thudding shut. I picked it up and threw it again. This time it hit a mess of books and boxes in the hallway and sprayed them with wayward raindrops.

When my breathing settled down, I slung my coat onto a hook and left it weeping into the puddle of water forming beneath it. I moved into the kitchen, leaving a trail of water worms from the tips of my shoelaces behind me. The noise of water gushing from the tap and crashing into the kettle sounded like it was relayed through a megaphone. When did these everyday sounds become so noticeable?

My mother's death had taken my sense of home and hearth away from me and all I wanted at that moment was to wrap myself in her presence. Tears slid from the corners of my eyes and by the time the flood became a trickle, both sleeves of my jumper were soaked from wiping my eyes and nose. Something like needles of ice started running along my spine. I switched the column heater on full blast.

Just then, a loud knock at the door jolted me into the present as if I'd charged into an unseen iron railing. A thin voice called out, 'Anna, Anna, it's only me!' – my Mum's neighbour, old Mrs Daly. I s'pose she's *my* neighbour now.

I managed to croak, 'Just a minute.' I quickly splashed some water on my face and ran my fingers through my hair as I ran to open the door.

Mrs Daly stood on the doorstep in an oversize mac. The edge of the hood settled at the bottom edge of her eyebrows and left only two eye slits peering at me above a wide toothy grin. The front of the coat was wrapped around what could've been a giant pumpkin or, in a much younger woman, a baby at the end of gestation.

'Hello, luv. Wild night. Brought you some nourishment.'

I snickered at the sight of her. She bustled in, placed a basket on the table and started pulling plates and bowls from a cupboard, like she'd been doing regularly over the past few months.

'Anna, you been cryin' again, luv. That's good. Cryin's better that that numb nothingness I've seen in your face these past weeks. D'you mind if I stay here a while and we'll have a bite to eat together?'

While she spoke, she lifted three dishes from the box. I could smell something savoury. Steam rose from the biggest dish.

'That'll be fine. I…there's nothing… I didn't stop at the shops… Give me your wet coat. Yours and mine can drip together.'

A visit from Mrs Daly was like switching my iPod shuffle on to 'random' – you never knew what to expect but it was always pleasant and comforting.

The kitchen warmed up. I slipped off to my room and peeled off wet jeans, jumper, socks and shoes and plunged into the comfort of my old track suit and ski socks. I caught a glimpse of splotches on my face in the mirror – it looked like the face of an adolescent fighting hormonal adjustment. I thought I heard the mirror say 'Who's not drinking their water then, missy?' Just like Mum used to say.

When I got back to the kitchen, the table had been set and the kettle was whistling away.

'Thanks heaps, Mrs Daly. I really appreciate this.'

'It's no trouble at all, Anna. I've been wanting to have a wee talk with you about what you're going to do now. I mean, are you going to stay on here by yourself or what?' She stared into my eyes as she fired the questions at me.

'Don't know yet, Mrs Daly. Can't make up my mind about that.'

'D'you think you could start calling me Lettie like your ma did? I mean ,it's so much easier to say.' She giggled.

After years of neighbourly good turns from Mum, Mrs Daly's generosity was not unexpected, but I wondered how such a big kind heart could fit into this diminutive body.

Soup, thick with chunks of ham straight from the bone, barley and lentils, carrots, leeks, and potatoes warmed me to the core. Then we sat with our hands around mugs of hot chocolate, picking into pastry filled with spicy apples and sultanas.

'Mardi has asked me to move into the house she shares with Augie and Joe. She thinks that being among people my own age will keep me motivated and get me back on track with my studies.'

During the past weeks I'd lain awake in the night seeing the darkness around me as the mouth of a huge engulfing fear. At those times, I was tempted to take up Mardi's offer.

Lettie looked puzzled as if she was pushing buttons on her memory bank. Her eyes widened. 'Holy mother of Jesus! Is she the one I saw staggering drunk and jumping into your pool at one of your birthday parties?' She slapped her hands to her face in consternation.

The incident had been two years before when Mardi first moved to Adelaide from Victoria. She'd splashed around while singing 'Happy birthday to you' in top pitch.

'Yup, that's Mardi,' I said. 'She's truly been a reliable and caring friend to me.'

'Reliable?' Lettie raised her eyebrows. 'Don't know about that. Caring? – maybe, but you need to be looked after, Anna, and you need direction and I can't see you getting that in a share house. But you'll no doubt make up your own mind. All I can say at this time is mind how you go, and if you decide to move, I'll expect regular phone calls and a visit now and again.'

'Thanks Mrs D…I mean Lettie… I appreciate your concern. It's just that I hate coming home to an empty house and Augie's place has energy bursting from the walls with music and chatter. That's one side of it, but my mother provided a comfortable home here for me and moving seems like a silly, impractical idea.'

'Now you're talking sense,' Lettie said, wiping crumbs of pastry from the table.

We cleaned up the dishes and packed her basket with empty bowls and plates.

'Well, goodnight, Anna luv. Remember, I'm only next door any time you need company or a good meal.'

For a while after that, I watched raindrops slide like silver snails down the window panes. The trees and plants in the back yard caught my attention – so many shades of green. With the help of security lights that Mum had installed after Dad died, the movement of branches and leaves changed wet silvery tones to greens of a translucent new-leaf tint. I started to count the different shades of green. Apple. Jade. Bottle. Sage. Olive.

Emerald green shining on the wet leaves of a ginger plant reminded me of a slinky, silk shawl Dad had bought Mum in the Irish shop in the city. Compared to the tints on the foliage, the pale shade on the cornices above me looked more like the 'snot green' of Joyce's sea in *Ulysses*. Thinking of that reminded me that a neglected backlog of reading and writing waited in a box in a corner of my study. But after Lettie's company and the food she'd brought, I felt like I could tackle a bit more sorting of the clutter in the hall.

I began stretching my body in every direction. I coaxed myself through a series of yoga movements – dog stretches, salute to the sun. Kneeling on the wooden floor was sore on my hands and knees. It reminded me of things I'd read about penitents and hair shirts in earlier times but the action and deep breathing energised me.

The phone rang. Mardi: 'Put the kettle on, see you in ten.'

When Mum first got sick and I couldn't get to lectures, Mardi had helped me by picking up books and returning them to the uni library. Sometimes she'd been my note-taking proxy at lectures.

**6**

During the weeks since Mum died, I'd been clearing out her clothes and crying a lot as I caught the scent of her from things she'd worn a few short weeks before. I found a box of old clothes Mum had kept for dress up games when I was little. Loud-checked pants flaring out to half a metre at the hem were creased and flattened by the weight of fitted body shirts, batik blouses, embroidered cheesecloth tunics and tie-dyed jeans.

Amongst all the stuff was a box of beaded necklaces, poppet beads and droopy filigree earrings. Each day since finding it, I had worn beads and earrings from the hoard as a conduit to the spirit of my mother. I began worrying the beads I'd put on that morning. Separate. Together. Separate…together…like a rosary.

Sitting cross-legged amongst the detritus of her life, I felt overwhelmed by the need to reach out and touch her. I needed to feel her hands stroke my back. Like she did when I'd been bent over books for hours. I grabbed a shawl from the pile and rocked myself through another crying session.

During this clean out, I'd taken boxes of papers and shelves of books from Mum's bedroom and stacked them in the hallway. I'd no idea what to do with them. While waiting for Mardi, I started poking through titles and authors, trying to focus on what should be done next.

I'd left the front door unlocked and was staring into space trying to focus on the shambles before me when Mardi bounced in fumbling with the collapsing mechanism of a wet yellow umbrella.

She called across the room, 'Hi, Anna. How are you?'

In a leather jacket over tight jeans, a shocking pink camisole top and a black silk shirt trimmed with gold chains, she looked like she was ready to party. Her hair was swirled on top; some wispy fronds had escaped and lay softly on glowing cheeks. She unwound a red scarf, about three metres long, from around her neck and nearly tripped over the mass of papers and books as she hung her jacket and scarf on a hook.

Comparing Mardi's glamorous get-up with my pilled and faded tracksuit, stringy hair, swollen eyes, I looked like one of those old bag ladies you might see in Rundle Mall.

'Need any help?' she said, crouching beside me. I could smell shampoo and Chanel No. 5. 'Tell you what, I'll make us a coffee then we'll see about talking, okay?' She disappeared into the kitchen.

It seemed like only seconds before her voice jolted me back to reality.

She stood halfway along the hall holding a tray of hot drinks and biscuits. 'Wanna have this in the kitchen?

'Aren't you going out?'

'I can go out anytime. It's only a bunch of people pubbing around. Why don't you clean yourself up and join us?'

The last time I'd gone to a club with Mardi, had been a strange and solitary experience for me. Although people milled around and the place was noisy with pub talk and cursing, I'd felt alone. Isolated. Like a stranger amongst the camaraderie.

'Thanks, but I really must tidy this stuff up then start on my studies. Dunno why I started. It's a mess.'

'What you wanna do, Anna, is make a list. Prioritise. Organise.'

'Yeah, right, Mardi. The theory's fine. You make a list and start at the top. But the problem with things is, they just sit there, defiant. They rule time and space and sap your energy. People and pets at least move one in a while. Things don't. '

'Okay. I get the message. I'll help you for a while.' Mardi picked her way through the books. She set the tray on the floor, kicked off her strappy patent shoes and sat down beside me. 'Would you rather have a Scotch or Bundy?' she asked, holding out a cup to me.

'No, Mardi, this is fine.'

'Anything you wanna talk about? Y'know, it might help. What's on your mind, Anna?'

'Nothing. I'm okay. Really I am…it's just that…'

Mardi started poking around boxes in a back corner. 'Hey! What's this?' She held up a couple of old LPs.

'It's a collection of old albums. Dad had a passion for garage sales. He was always buying junk of one kind or another.'

'Looks like these two are full of old Scottish songs. Wouldn't mind listening to some of them. D'you still have a turntable that works?'

I saw a gleam of excitement in her eyes. She was up to something.

'Don't know if it works. It's been gathering dust for years in the back room.'

Off she went, carrying the whole box full.

A few minutes later, she shouted out, 'Found it.'

Then I heard the scratchy sounds of accordion music followed by a Scottish voice singing an ancient ditty that I remembered from my childhood. When Dad played these songs, he and Mum used to march up and down arm in arm singing into each other's faces.

Mardi called out, 'Anna, come in here a minute.'

I struggled to my feet. There she was dancing a parody of the Highland Fling and laughing her head off.

'C'mon, Anna, let's sing along with the man. I'll play this track again.' She pulled me into the room.

The next thing I knew we were accompanying the voice of long-dead Harry Lauder with the lyrics of 'Roamin' in the Gloamin''. Mardi didn't know all the words but her exaggerated rrrrrrrr sound rang full and funny each time it came up and we burst out laughing. When she sang the last 'rrrrrrrroamin' in the gloamin'', she marched out to watch herself in the hall mirror, her shoulders and head moving to the rhythm of the music.

I laughed at her antics, then fell in a heap. She stood silent. I felt her arms around me.

'I'm so sorry. Anna. Wish I could….'

'Mardi, it's okay… I'm okay now. I just want this emotional see-saw to STOP!'

'Maybe all you need right now is a good long crying session.'

'Don't know what I need right now. I shouldn't have started reorganising things. I don't know if getting rid of Mum's stuff is the right thing to do.'

Mardi turned off the music. I sat on the floor and she made a space beside me.

'Time for a break. Let's talk about…your mum.'

My parents had lived in Australia since 1964. My father was English and Mum was Scottish and when I was little I used to ask them about grandparents or aunties and cousins. I'd heard other kids in school talking about these things or such people.

Dad would say, 'I've no relatives that I know of, but your mum has two brothers somewhere in the UK. You've probably got cousins and aunties but we never hear from them.'

Mum told me she'd no idea where her brothers lived. She'd say these things with pursed lips and look at Dad the way people do when they share a secret.

They never tired of telling me about their early days in Adelaide and the fun they'd had finding accommodation and jobs. But it seemed to me that, other than snippets about gardening and their voyage to Australia, their life before that was a series of blank pages. How strange it felt, to be in some kind of time capsule speeding towards their past. En Route to London I read some more.

**8**

### 28 March 2007

*My mother comes through the shadows more often now and sometimes, in my mind, I try to reconcile with her. But always something pushes itself between us, leaving her at one side of the barrier and me at the other. It isn't like we're opposing each other as we did when I was young; it's more like a wall keeps us from seeing the truth of each other.*

### 29 March 2007

*My mother used to say I'd see the devil in the mirror one day and when I look at the reflection of my drawn pasty face, I wonder if that's what she meant – and I wonder if she's changed from the days when prayer and penance were the only cures she knew. Does she still see Hell in the ground beneath her feet, and the sky above her head as the doorway to Heaven? Back then she trampled over my feelings the way people rampage over footprints on Australian beaches.*

### 3 April 2007

*Tonight waiting and listening for the sound of Anna's key in the door. She'll probably make some tea and sit on my bed here beside me. I'll tell her about some of the characters that lived in the village where I grew up.*

*I'll tell her about summer evenings in my childhood when we played in the gloaming – so different from southern summers where darkness falls in the time it takes to drive from the corner of our street to the driveway. Back then, the children of Vale Street would gather on the oval and entertain their parents with songs and dancing. We'd dress up like princesses, or villains, or brides and we'd act out some drama that had been written in a hurry or sing the songs we'd heard on the hit parade.*

## 10 April 2007

*The mirror tells the honest truth of my condition. My face has changed, particularly my eyes. They stare back at me like small hard jet beads. I turn my head this way and that, thinking I'll look better in another light. It's worse. It's the face of an old, old woman. I feel my soul shrinking as the disease takes over – like a sponge being squeezed tight with a hand stronger than mine.*

*I am learning more and more about my body. Each day new limitations present themselves and new challenges confront me. Yesterday, I learned that if I lie still and breathe as deeply as I can for a few minutes, I have stored enough energy to shower and dress myself without help. But despite my best efforts I am growing weaker.*

*Now, fits of panic, fits of crying, fits of anger consume me and I find it strange that my illness makes no difference to the rest of the world. People still catch the 137 bus to the city. Shops still fill with customers searching for dresses and dishes.*

*It's like the night Anna was born when Peter shouted the news to the world from a hospital window. Then he turned to me, eyes squinting, shoulders shrugging and said, 'Y'know what, Eleanor? Nobody's listening.'*

## 3rd May 2007

*Lately I've been thinking more and more about Scotland. The people, the smells, the food, the softness of the air. I am besieged with longing for the sound of the voices. Is this what dying is all about? Time, when I look back on my life with Peter, seems to have gone very quickly and as smoothly as the water curving over a weir in a polished flow without break or interruption.*

*I remember things now that I haven't thought about in years – like Fiona and me running away from home, and the good times we had in our teenage years. Dear, generous Fiona, I wonder if life has been kind to her.*

## *11 May 2007*

*While waiting for Anna to come home, I called Telstra's International Assistance and asked if they could find me a Glenhill phone number for Mr James Kennedy, Fiona's father. The operator's voice said the only listing for Kennedy at that address was for Ms Fiona Kennedy and within a few minutes Fiona and I were crying over the phone to each other. I laughed between the tears when she said, 'Jeez, Elner…don't hear from you in thirty odd years and you're still cryin' – like you were the last time I saw you. Hope you've had some laughs between bawlin' sessions.' Then she told me that she and Jimmy Bogle had been married but divorced years ago and she'd changed her name back to her birth name. She said it would be great to see me again and asked why I didn't come home for a wee holiday. I told her that that wasn't possible, not that I didn't want to. When she asked why, I quickly changed the subject. I didn't have the heart to tell her about the cancer.*

*I asked her did she remember the time we ran away to London and the day we went to Dunoon and I met Peter and she said, 'How could I forget, Elner? You were havin' such a great time an' I was such a misery.'*

*I can't believe that she still lives across the oval. She inherited the house from her parents when they died. And my parents still live in the house where I'd last seen them. Nothing seems to have changed since I last saw the place.*

*As I write this, echoes of the things we'd talked about weave around in my mind. I can see Fiona and me, dressed to the nines going off to the pictures or dancing and giggling about how the old people in the village put in their days. We were so cocky, we thought we'd live forever. She promised not to talk about the phone call to anyone in the village, especially my parents.*

*I can hear Anna coming up the driveway – hope she doesn't see signs of my tears.*

**9**

That was the last entry. I closed the diary, put it in my flight bag and thought about a morning just after that date. I'd been lying on top of Mum's bed. We were silent. It was just after dawn, and the room was already light. I'd opened the curtains to let the sun stream in. She'd turned away from the brightness. I'd left her to her own thoughts and started making breakfast. I defrosted some blueberries, and put them with bowls of breakfast cereal and mugs of coffee on a tray. When I came back to her room, she'd smiled at me. The talk went like this.

'I'm feeling better this morning, Anna – better than I've felt in weeks.'

'That's great, Mum. I've made your favourite breakfast.'

'Just leave it for now, love, and fetch me my old gardening clothes.'

'Nope. Not until you've had something to eat.'

She grumbled about my stubborn streak. 'You inherited that from your father, y'know. He'd never give way in an argument.'

'So you've told me – a million times.'

'I want to dig my hands into the soil and smell the greenness around me.'

'Okay, Mum, so long as you don't overdo it.'

'Y'know, Anna, my dad used to whistle and sing as he worked in the garden. He taught me how to plant seeds and care for the new shoots of carrots and I remember seeing tiny new shoots of sweet peas climbing along a trellis on the wall of the garden hut.'

I looked straight into her eyes. 'I'd like you to tell me about your father. My grandfather.'

'Perhaps I'll tell you one day. For now, all I'm saying is he was a good man.'

After we ate, I helped her get dressed. I had to tie her too-big jeans around her waist with a soft belt. While I tidied up her room and gathered my books together, I could hear her singing softly. I looked out, and watched her choose bulbs from an old basket and place them around the Queensland brush box tree that she and Dad had planted the week they'd moved into the house. I didn't know what flowers the bulbs would bring, but I hoped that, whatever they were, we'd both be around in September to see them bloom.

I'd picked up my backpack and looked out to say goodbye.

Just then, she shouted 'Annaaagh, Annaaagh!' as if she was choking on something.

I ran to her side. She fell into my arms, sagging like Raggedy Ann. She'd lost so much weight it was no trouble at all to lift her up like a baby and carry her inside. After giving her two morphine tablets, I phoned her doctor.

When I settled her in bed again and before she'd drifted off to sleep she whispered, 'I hope you take a trip back to Scotland, Anna.'

'We'll go together.'

'No, darling, you go. You'll have a better time without me.' By the time she'd finished talking, her voice had faded and her eyelids drooped.

I left her to sleep and dream about flowers and fecundity in a garden thousands of miles away.

*

My thoughts were interrupted by the flight attendant unlatching the table on the seat in front. She placed a tray of food on it and asked what I'd like to drink. I felt tired. Reading Mum's story left me drained. As if some power had sucked every gram of energy from my body and left an empty shell in its wake. The sight of chicken sitting in a gluggy satay sauce turned my appetite off. Completely. I slept. I dreamt.

Black gowns and academic headpieces crowded me out of some

kind of melee. Someone handed me a rolled-up parchment. When I unrolled it I saw my mother's name written in scintillating cursive gold lettering. Nothing else. A hand with no body attached placed a tiny bunch of rosemary in the palm of my hand.

The rattle of the dinner tray startled me awake.

'I'm so sorry,' the attendant said. 'Didn't you feel like eating? Would you like me to get you a sandwich?'

I shrugged 'No.'

# 10

## Adelaide

Looking like before and after shots for a makeover ad, Mardi and I sorted the books and stacked them in a corner.

'Let's make a list of your priorities,' Mardi said, and reached into her bag for a biro and paper.

'Well, first I gotta find my binders and folders with assignment notes. Then I need to phone uni to get extensions. Then I need to re-read Book 1 of *Paradise Lost*, plus all my notes on that and my notes on *Ulysses*.'

Since the beginning of my Honours year, I'd been concentrating on the writings of Milton and Joyce. They'd challenged and intrigued me and demanded more time than I'd been able to give. Two assignments were overdue and another paper from the Great Texts of Western Civilisation course was due in six weeks. I'd missed so many lectures I was on the brink of withdrawing.

Mardi scribbled. 'Good, that's a real step forward… Next?'

'That's enough for now, Mardi. If I can get some of this mess cleaned up, I'll be happy.'

When I'd cleaned out Mum's wardrobe, I'd found an old suitcase stashed behind travelling bags and old hat boxes. I'd left it unopened, intending to look through it some other time.

'What's in that old suitcase? Mardi asked. 'You wanna put it away somewhere?'

'Don't know what's in it. By the look of the rust on the locks it's prob'ly full of junk from years ago… Haven't found a key that fits.'

'Let's open it. If it's just rubbish, you can put it on the back porch until next hard refuse day. But we might get a laugh from the stuff inside.'

Mardi fiddled with the locks – tapping with her fingernails – trying to get some kind of movement, then she started waving her hands around. 'Bloody hell, Anna, look!' She held out her hands. Most of her fingers looked like she'd dipped them in a pot of ochre paint.

I smiled at her annoyance. 'Maybe just leave it for now, Mardi.'

'No way. I'm much too connected to the thing now to let it sit here.'

She found a screwdriver in the kitchen catch-all drawer and rubber gloves by the sink. We lugged the suitcase to the middle of the floor. With a turn of the screw, the locks broke free and we pulled the lid off. A mouldy smell hit my nostrils.

'Yeugh!'

Mardi countered, 'Smells like something's growing between the layers.'

The case was full to the brim with magazines, sewing patterns and greeting cards. Mardi picked out a card the size of a tabloid newspaper. It had padded satin covers with faded roses and handwriting on every available space.

'Listen to this, Anna: "For years without number, / My heart's been in a slumber / But now that you're here, / I love you most dear." And look, Anna, hearts and arrows and hugs and kisses all over the place! And here's another: "Roses are red, violets are blue. Do you like to dance? I do too." Can't believe adult people actually wrote these things to each other. Can you?'

'Nope, but that was when Mum and Dad were silly teenagers.'

We giggled and sniggered and laughed till our jaws ached.

I picked up a buff-coloured envelope with newspaper clippings attached to it with a bulldog clip. Black headlines dated 1963 were clear enough to read:

The U.S Navy Conquers Holy Loch

Ban the Bomb

Protesters Demand Nuclear Disarmament

Captions beside creased faces were yellowed by time and mainly illegible. I distinguished odd phrases about rebels being arrested next to faded pictures of crowd scenes. I handed them to Mardi and tore the envelope open. A letter and photos spilled onto the floor. The letter was in Dad's handwriting, dated May 1964 and addressed to Mum at an address in Oban, Scotland. In one paragraph it said,

> I wish I'd told you sooner how I really feel about you and then maybe this wouldn't have happened. You must be some strong person to take the stand you have in the face of the opposition.
>
> What can I do to help you get through this time? I want to jump on the first train and come to your side and kiss your pain away. I am so sorry for your troubles.

It ended with a quote from Yeats that I knew and loved:

> But one man loved the pilgrim soul in you
> And loved the sorrows of your changing face.

I placed the paper flat on the kitchen table and tried to recall times when my parents said loving words to each other. Tried to remember things they'd told me about their early days together. But I couldn't remember them saying anything as beautiful as these elegant words. I read the letter again and my heart filled with emptiness.

Mardi handed me the small black and white snapshots. 'Look at the names on the back, Anna.'

The first photo showed a man and a woman standing in front of a garden looking straight into the camera. The man had a soft cap tilted to the back of his head and the woman wore a patterned dress (it could've been floral), nipped at the waist with a wide belt. They stood apart from each other like people do when they've disagreed about something. The details were blurred but their faces looked solemn, the way people used to look when they posed for passport photos. A group shot showed the same man and woman with two tall men beside them who looked to be in their twenties. They were dressed in cricket whites, shin guards and fat gloves. They each had a cricket bat in one hand and held their other hand up as if they were waving to someone beyond the camera. They were smiling great toothy grins. The inscription on the back in delicate cursive writing said: The McCraes of Glenhill. Mum, Dad, Andy and Jack. Remember us Ellie. June 1964.

I'd never heard anyone call my mother Ellie, even in the lightest moments between them, Dad had always used Eleanor. Other photos showed the older man standing on a bridge with a church in the background, near a river and another of him in a country lane holding up what could've been fruit of some kind. I stared at the faces. Could this be Mum's two brothers and the older couple my grandparents. Was this the family she'd never talked about? My family?

I looked again and read the letter once more. What was the trouble mentioned? What terrible thing had happened to my mother? She'd never told me about anything sinister in her life.

'I'm stunned Mardi. It looks like I might have family. I mean, the young men in this one look like…they might be still alive. I'm dumbstruck! I wonder which one is Jack and which one is Andy?'

Mardi said, 'Uncle Andy McCrae, Uncle Jack McCrae,' and the sound of the names lay feathersoft on my ears, like some forgotten familiar words.

Mardi started putting on her shoes. She stepped over the suitcase then stopped. With one shoe in her hand she turned to me. 'I don't think you should be alone right now Anna. How about coming over to Augie's place and we'll cook up something tasty. Maybe have a game of Trivial Pursuit or something. Joe, the new fella, is a lot of fun. I'm sure getting out of this mess for a while will…'

'Thanks Mardi, but no. Not tonight. Maybe some other time.'

'Well how 'bout I call them to come over here?'

'Mardi, I'd really rather be alone. I appreciate your help and your kindness but I want to be alone to think.'

'Okay. If you're sure. You've got my number so if you change your mind about company ring me. You know I'm here for you twenty four seven.' She gathered her things together and moved to the door calling back to me with an encouraging smile, 'I'll check with you tomorrow.'

'Have a good time Mardi, thanks.'

As she stood at the open door, I saw sheets of rain like steel barbs shining under the street light. When I heard the sound of her car move away I nearly ran after it to wave her back.

The feeling around me was like a room sometimes is at the end of a party when the revellers have gone and all that is left of them is half-filled snack dishes and empty glasses. Ghostly.

I read Dad's letter again and stared at the McCrae's faces for a minute or two before putting everything back in the suitcase, closing the lid and shoving it into a corner.

## 11

The next afternoon Mardi arrived. 'Fancy a walk?' she asked.

'Yeah…sure…good timing. I'll get my jacket.'

We walked along the linear park that followed the course of the river. The air was full of fragrances. Lemon. Eucalyptus. Pine tickled my nose. Shady spots blotted out the sun and my face tingled in patches of cold air. Sounds of bicycle bells and broken bits of conversation from passing walkers mixed with birdsong to give the illusion of early summer.

As we walked, Mardi talked about her job.

'D'you think you'll stay with Flight Centre forever?' I asked.

'No way. As soon as I've saved enough, I'm off overseas.'

'Where?'

'Prob'ly London. Thousands of Aussies are having a great time going off to Europe, tasting the beer in Dubrovnik…Prague… Cologne. Imagine having a drink in a pub five hundred years old!'

'Where would you stay? How would you get work?'

'The daughter of one of the men in my office lives in London. She does bar work and she's forever going off to Europe. She did a six-week course on Renaissance art in Florence and a summer school at Oxford on Renaissance literature. Me? I just wanna travel. I'm sick of booking people up for great adventures – time I had one of my own.'

Since reading about the civil wars of the seventeenth century, it had been my ambition to see places like St Paul's Cathedral where Archbishop Laud and John Donne had preached. And Bread Street where Milton was born and the streets around Cheapside where he'd walked and talked with Dryden and Marvell.

'You're dreaming again Anna,' Mardi said, pulling me out of a cyclist's path.

'Maybe one day, I'll study at Oxford,' I said, 'or maybe London University, where history happened.'

'For that, you'll have to get serious about your study.'

'I know that.'

'It'd be fantastic if we could meet in London. We'd do the theatres and take a sail down the Thames to Greenwich. I've checked out websites for pubs all over Europe. In England they have the weirdest names like the Pope's Grotto. Imagine the Pope havin' a pub!'

I laughed at her enthusiasm and antics.

She stopped walking and talking, looked at me and said, 'it's so good to hear you laugh, Anna, and it's great to see some colour in your face.'

I realised then that while we'd been walking, I'd unloaded some of my grief – like I'd taken off a heavy coat and left it somewhere out of sight.

We spent an hour over drinks in a café chatting about Mardi's job, my studies and the latest movies. When we were ready to leave, she told me that Augie and Joe had invited us to a barbecue. Augie held yoga classes in a studio attached to his house. I'd been to some of his sessions and I knew him quite well but I hadn't yet met Joe.

'What's Joe like?'

'He's…mmm…well, he's different from anyone you'll ever meet. He's a geologist working for an oil company and often goes off on field trips. We often don't see him for weeks at a time.'

# 12

When we arrived at Augie's place, it looked like the house was on fire. Smoke belched from a wok on the stove and streamed through the open front door. Joe, arms waving, head turned sideways and face screwed up tight, looked like he was at the losing end of a salvage operation to save chunks of charcoal. Augie stood beside him waving a fly swat with one hand and holding a bottle of beer in the other.

'Hi!' Joe said. 'You Anna? How ya doin'? The fuckin' barbecue doesn't work. Hope you like your chicken black.' A tangle of frizzy ringlets around his face looked like they'd been sewn onto the woolly hat meeting his eyebrows and smelling like wet dog. A stringy beard tried to cover his chin, and the woolly jumper he wore reached to his knees. It had the same burnt smell as the chicken in the wok.

Augie made his speciality, a crispy Thai salad. Mardi brought a fruit and cheese platter. In the end, the chicken got turfed into the bin along with the wok. After rummaging in the fridge, Joe found some vegetarian patties and heated them in the microwave. We shuffled and bumped our way around the kitchen table and onto rickety wooden chairs.

Joe's long arms seemed to take up half the table. While we ate, he told us he'd been digging for 'fuckin fossils on Kangaroo Island'. Then he started drumming his fingers on the table. Drrrm…drrrm…drrrm, slap, slap…as if he was beating a bongo drum. 'I've been working with a bunch o' fuckin' morons for the past three weeks,' he moaned, clutching his head.

Mardi said, 'Pay no attention to him, Anna. He's really a sweetie.'

'Hey, Joe,' Augie said, picking up a bit of paper from a pile on a little table behind him. 'Listen to this. Maybe you should stick it on the windscreen when you're driving to the next site.' He quoted, 'See the happy moron. / He doesn't give a damn. / I wish I were a moron… my God! / Perhaps I am!'

We screeched with laughter. Joe threw his beanie across the table at Augie. It missed and landed on the cat's dish, where Augie had thrown some leftover food. I imagined the smell settling amongst the threads of the hat, attracting stray animals that would follow Joe, like the rats that followed the Pied Piper.

When the hilarity died down, Joe looked sheepish. 'They're not a bad bunch really,' he said. 'Three weeks is just too long in the field and I need a decent night's sleep.'

As if the sun heard our laughter and Joe's speech of contrition, it bounced through the windows and spread over the room, linking us together. I felt the wound in my soul close a little bit more.

# 13

It was late when I got home but I felt better than I had in a long while. I sat in front of my computer and thought about Joe. His smile. The blueness of his eyes. And how good it felt to laugh again. A feeling of guilt about my work intruded into this warmth so I clicked the start button and typed: 'Discuss the Political Message of *Paradise Lost*', printed it, and stuck it facing me across the top of the monitor.

I leafed through chapter headings and indices of historical texts. I picked up my copy of *Paradise Lost*. When I got to the line '…justify the ways of God to men', I tossed it at my feet. The cursor on the screen blinked and dared me to start writing. I pressed a button – shut it down and found an anthology of short stories amongst Mum's books. Before heading for bed, I stuck out my tongue at the dead monitor, and felt all-powerful. After two paragraphs blessed sleep turned my eyes off.

# 14

Early next morning when I walked along the riverside track I stopped to watch a family of ducks. One duck stood alone at the water's edge. I saw lumps like globules of pus stuck between its toes and halfway up its foot. It had trouble waddling and stood apart from its family. I wanted to pick it up and take it home but decided I'd be better off going home and searching for the half-written essays I'd buried somewhere amongst my things.

After a quick breakfast, I rang uni to make an appointment with Doc Wallace.

When we connected, his voice boomed in my ear. 'Good to hear from you, Anna. How can I help?'

'I'd like to meet with you to…'

He didn't let me finish. 'Can you be here before eleven-thirty?

'Sure.'

Before setting off along the bike track, I searched CDs and USB files but gave up after half an hour and settled for a few pages of handwritten drafts and notes and stuffed them in my backpack.

## 15

The Unicoff café buzzed with the sounds of lunch time. Students huddled, debated and disputed. Bags lay open under tables covered with papers on disparate subjects. Voices were soft and loud, shrieking and secretive in a crucible filled with unfinished sentences and occasional loud laughter.

'Did you believe…?'

'Nothing but the original…'

'I need to concentrate…'

'What? No!'

'I'm not saying he's right or wrong…'

Spilled drinks. Careful carriers of salads, chips and chocolate cake. Posters advertising Black Stallion drink, Pizza Haven, Coca Cola and Unirecords decorated the walls. The digital 'ding' of cash registers accompanied the rattle and crash of dispensing machines. Smells of bread, fried finger food, sweat and coffee overlaid recess activities. A young fair Adonis flaunted a T-shirt broadcasting, 'For a good lay call Candy's Carpets'. Smokers braved wintry weather on the veranda for a final cigarette before classes.

Dr Wallace bustled across the cafeteria butting into chairs and catching his outside-in raincoat on table corners. I smiled at this image of someone I knew to be composed and in control on a dais.

'Some fool left the sprinkler on,' he blustered. 'I'm wetter from walking through that than the rain.' He pulled a wrinkled hankie from an inside pocket and wiped his face. Some drips fell onto papers he'd slapped onto the table. 'Would you like a hot chocolate or coffee?'

'No, thanks. Just had one. Thank you for taking the time to see me.' He plonked onto a chair opposite me and I showed him the dog-eared drafts of two essays.

'This is all I could find.'

All he said was 'Hmph' and picked up the crumpled pages by the corner as if they carried a contagion.

By the time he spoke to me again, my habit of picking at the skin on the back of my hands had reached a state of agitation.

'Looks like you've a lot of work ahead of you, Anna, but I'm confident in your ability to get through it. Now, what's your plan?'

I handed him three extension forms.

'Tell you what,' he whispered as if we were in some kind of conspiracy, 'I'll sign two for the work you've already started. When you've handed them in, I'll sign the third one for your major paper. Are you happy with that?' He looked over his glasses at me.

I crossed my fingers before promising I'd meet the deadlines he set.

'Contact me any time you need to discuss your work.' He gathered up his things and was halfway across the room before scurrying back. 'Here's a list of resources you might find useful. The Christopher Hill book is particularly concise.' He charged through the crowds again.

I found most of the texts he'd recommended in the library and cycled home along the bike track, breezing through the trees, enjoying an occasional flight on downhill stretches. I hardly noticed the weight of books on my back.

# 16

During the weeks that followed, I read and wrote. I deleted and re-wrote. Phrases and facts jostled through my head like ants in a crack of paving. I'd hardly time to compose them onto the screen. I read everything I could get my hands on about religious intolerance and secular supremacy in the seventeenth century.

It seemed to me that Milton had garnered the insight required to write about these things from the turbulent times he lived in. With lines like 'Earth felt the wound…all was lost', he presented images of profound sadness. The realisation that some human beings needed to abuse those who trod a different path to their perception of God disturbed me. I felt privileged to be living in better times and wondered how me and the house mates would've fitted in to the ethos of seventeenth-century England. Would Joe take sides? Which side?

Wheels of ideas spun in my head. Each afternoon I'd arrive home, change into my tracksuit, switch on the computer and type like a crazy person. Or I'd sit in Mum's chair with a stack of resources beside me and read until past midnight.

It took no time at all to over-reach my word target for each day. My entire world was about writing, researching and cycling back and forth for lectures. At times when I felt drained, I'd stare at pages of paragraphs or into space as though I was in a vacuum.

Mrs Daly – Lettie – had a key to my house and often when I'd come home, chicken salad or a casserole with heating instructions waited for me. And a yellow post-it note stuck on the fridge signified a special treat inside.

A note came from Joe: 'I love the way you care about your work – stay cool – Joe.'

If I thought about Mum, it was seeing her as a driving force with images of her bringing me a mug of hot chocolate, making me stop for a minute while she stroked my back and massaged my cramping fingers.

Mardi arrived one night with a plate laden with Chinese food from Joe. 'He says you gotta eat. He misses you.'

'He could've phoned. Where is he?'

'He got a call to go out bush somewhere and left in a hurry. Says he'll call you when he gets back.'

A note wrapped around the chopsticks said he'd be away on a dig until the end of October and when he got back 'we'll party for a week, like normal people do'.

At last, with a day to spare, I put the last dot on the final page, gave the whole thing one last scan and printed it.

Done.

Papers submitted.

Books returned to the library.

Rejected drafts shredded.

'Way to go!' I yelled to the walls.

I spent the next few days shifting the last of my mother's stuff. The books I delivered to the aged care centre. Other papers I put in the recycle bin. Gradually the house took on some order and no longer looked like a hurricane had swept through it.

The old suitcase still sat in the corner. It seemed to be calling out to me, as if the McCraes had acquired voices.

Next day I sent off an application for a scholarship course at London University. Now I had space to do normal things…like eat.

I invited Lettie to lunch at the Central Market. I bought sushi, smoked salmon, cheeses, a few bottles of wine and wood-oven bread to take home.

Later that day, while I was cleaning up the back porch, Mardi phoned to say Joe had come back earlier than expected. 'He's desperate to see you,' she giggled.

'He'll need to tell me that himself,' I sniggered back to her.

'Okay, I'll tell him that. See you around eight.'

'Don't you dare!' I yelled at her but she'd hung up.

I phoned Lettie. 'Some friends are coming over,. Would you like to join us?

'Oh no, Anna, you're all much too noisy for my liking. Besides I had a lovely time with you earlier. Have a good time with your pals. You deserve it.'

Augie, Mardi and Joe arrived just as the sun was setting. We feasted until late. When they were about to leave, Joe hung back. He stuttered a few words of thanks then gathered me in his arms for a long warm hug before stomping off.

**17**

On an early December morning, I walked on the beach in my bare feet letting the edge of the sea swirl around my ankles. Slivers of light where the sun caught the knife edge of surface activity looked like thousands of silver whiting speeding through the water.

I followed a family for a few metres – a man, a woman and a little girl. Each parent clasped a hand of the child, lifting her high and swinging her forward. The breeze caught the girl's hair and held the locks flowing like streams of gold behind her. When I heard their laughter, I wanted to make my world a little younger to a time when I'd been a little girl with Mum and Dad beside me.

At this time of year, Mum and I would usually be packing our bags for summer at Victor Harbor, and she'd be saying, 'Let's go shopping for bathers' or 'I'd like to see a movie with you'…the good end-of-year things.

I stopped in my tracks. Stricken. I heard her voice – as clear as if she stood beside me. Sunglasses hid my eyes and a shady spot by warm rocks sheltered me until the tears stopped.

While nursing my soul, I spotted a man loping along the beach. His hair stood on end like leafless twigs and he moved easily in his body. It was Joe. As he flew past me at the water's edge, I watched his long legs devour the distance. His upper body shone with sweat and I thought I saw sparks shoot from his arms as he ran. He was smiling. I didn't call out. I wanted to see him as the rest of the world could see him. I wanted to enjoy watching his body move. I wanted a memory to keep in my heart.

On the way home with the sun behind me, I followed my silent shadow.

That afternoon, with not a whisper of any living voice around me, I took another look at the McCrae family photos and newspaper articles in the old suitcase and for fun decided to do a Google search for Scotland and the Polaris protests at Dunoon in 1963. I passed an hour or so reading through hundreds of sites about 'one of the most active and sustained campaigns of protest in modern British history'.

Hmmmm…1963? The year The Beatles took over the music world. Woodstock was still an idea. So, where does this all fit into my mother's story?

One journalist reported,

History was made today when hundreds of onlookers, mostly men wearing duffle coats and armbands showing the CND symbol, lined the shoreline at Dunoon. I saw a tractor pulling a trailer carrying four or five students from Glasgow University on top of a stack of canoes. It stalled in a side street to let people pass. Someone from the crowd called out, 'Where ye headed? D'ye need more manpower?' And two scallywags scrambled aboard. Later I watched this same group in yellow jackets skim across the water towards the entrance to Holy Loch where the American ship USS *Hunley*, the focus of the protest, sat low in the water. People on the shore waved banners to cheer on their brave and reckless counterparts. A line of official launches flying the American ensign at their stern was strung across the narrow gorge blocking access to the loch. A red-haired lout shouted from a turned up orange crate, 'We're being subjected to risks of contamination and annihilation!' Families with young children were jostled to the back of the crowd.

I couldn't remember ever hearing my parents talk about these things.

When Joe and Mardi dropped in later, I showed them the articles I'd printed off.

Joe: 'Mebbe your old man was one of the protesters.'

'Don't think so, Joe. My dad was such a softy. He'd never get that angry.'

Mardi: 'Y'never know, Anna. He might have been a rebel in his young days. Anyway, somehow it's connected to the photos and clippings you've got. Why don't you do a search for the newspaper that printed the articles?'

I found a site for the *Paisley Daily Express* and sent an email to the editor listing the details from the photos, the address from the letter and asked if they could help me trace any of the McCrae family. I wasn't hopeful, given the scanty information on the ancient photos.

While I attached the email and printout to the other stuff, Joe poured us a glass of wine saying, 'Have you heard the one about the two Scots in a pub?'

Mardi raised her eyebrows and winked at me.

'Well, it's like this,' he started, 'two men sitting at the bar in a Glasgow pub. One says to the other, "Look, Jimmy, I can see a fly in your drink." Jimmy looks, sees the fly. He puts thumb and forefinger from both hands into the glass. He picks the fly up by the wings, shakes it and says, "Spit it oot, spit it oot!"' Joe laughed.

Mardi and I looked at him. 'Don't get it, Joe,' we said.

'Well, y'know how Scots are supposed to be tight-fisted...' His voice trailed away. Then he chortled. 'I've got another one, it's about...'

'Joe, I've got an early rise tomorrow so I gotta go. Save it for next time.'

Mardi put her shoes on and gathered up her bag and keys. Joe followed her to the door then turned back and hugged me. He was about to say something but changed his mind.

'See you later,' they called out.

Mardi shouted, 'Let us know how you go with the family thing.'

# 18

I'd forgotten about the email until I logged on a few days later. A message from the *Paisley Daily Express* said a woman in their office called Liz Morgan knew a family of McCraes and someone would be in touch with me. I printed the email and put it, with the letter and photos, in a file folder I labelled 'McCraes of Glenhill'. Next day, another email from Scotland:

Dear Anna,

My father, Andy McCrae (your mother's brother), asked me to contact you. He's got a computer but he only uses it to play FreeCell and Solitaire. Liz Morgan phoned Dad and you'd never believe how thrilled we all are to hear from you. We didn't know you existed. Dad nearly cried. He's been on the phone to Jack for over an hour. He wants to know how your mother is, and your dad. Where do you live? How did you find us? How old are you? Grandpa Malkie, (he's your grandpa too), will be ninety years old in July and we are planning a big celebration. He was so excited when we told him about your message. Please keep in touch and give yourself a big, big hug from all of us. Your cousin,

Claire McCrae

My cousin. Claire. Uncles. Grandparents. The knowledge swirled in my head. I wanted to sing and dance. The printer took such a long time to release the words into something I could touch and hold while I paced the floor and shouted to the ceiling, 'I have a family!'

I made myself a cup of tea and sat for a while on the back porch reading the email again and again. The words 'your grandpa too' shimmered and ruffled under my tears like hot daggers. What did my grandfather look like? Why hadn't my mother talked about them? I put the email in the folder with the other things. Later, riding along the riverside thinking about it, I felt clouds of grief steam away from me like fish under water.

I phoned Joe. He said, 'Fuckin' marvellous. That deserves a dinner out. Pick you up at seven.'

The restaurant was quietly busy. Subtle clinking of glasses. Whispered conversations. Mozart oozing in the background. Smells of fish, curry, steak.

'So,' Joe began when we were seated, 'tell me all.'

'Well, it's like this: it turns out I've got a family but they're on the other side of the world. What would you do about that?'

'Me? It's not my deal. I'm just getting a kick at the sight of your face smilin' for a change.'

'Have I been such a moron?'

'Nah, you've had a rough time. Anyway, what are your options here?'

'Not sure.'

'Maybe keep in touch but let the situation stew for a while.'

# 19

Before I went to bed that night, I emailed Claire and told her that Mum and Dad had both died.

Next morning, It seemed I'd hardly hit the send button on an email to Mardi when she phoned.

'What great news, Anna. How d'you feel about all that? I'm so excited for you!'

'I'm still trying to get my head around it all. I mean, why didn't Mum tell me about them?'

'Well, Anna, as you've often said to me, everything has a reason to it. Maybe your mum was, in her way, being protective.'

We talked for almost an hour.

Until now I'd been angry with Mum for dying on me. I understood this to be unadulterated grief, and I'd linked it to a mean destiny. Now, discovering that she had in a sense, wiped out whatever family I had, my anger became two-pronged. She knew she was dying. She had time to tell me about the McCraes. Why hadn't she?

Later that evening I sat for a while in Mum's chair remembering conversations we'd had about where we'd travel to when I'd finished my honours year. She'd show me around the place of her birth. 'One day you and I will climb McCaig's Folly in Oban,' she'd said so many times. And I imagined we'd arrive breathless at the top and she'd tell me about a time in the past when she'd climbed those same steps, watched similar scenes. Why all this talk about Scotland but nothing about her brothers or parents? I thought about the last word I heard my mother say a few days before she sunk into a coma. I'd brought her a spray of cymbidium orchids from our garden. She looked at them through half-closed eyes and said, 'Lovely.' Nothing more.

I wanted to shake her back to me. I wanted to see her sitting curled in her chair where I now sat. I wanted to ask more questions about Scotland. I wanted to ask her about the people in the photos.

The next day I received this from Claire:

Dear Anna,

We are all so sorry to hear that your mum and dad have died. Grandpa was sad. He spent a long time in the hut. I think he cried —we couldn't hear him whistling or singing like he usually does. It must be hard for you being on your own now. Well, you're not really on your own – a tribe of people wait here, dying to meet you. It would be wonderful if you could come to Scotland at some stage – you'd be most welcome. I want you to fall in love with the place then you might come home and stay for a while. Try the websites electricscotland or visitrannoch.

Gran and Granpa's address is 86 Hart St, Glenhill, Renfrewshire, Scotland PA5 345.

Cheerio for now.

Claire

When I read this message it seemed to me that I knew Claire. Her voice came clear and strong through the printed words of welcome.

**20**

Over the next few days exploring websites about Scotland focused my thoughts and kept me busy. It sent me on a trail through mountains and moors. I read about superstitions and learned that urisks and kelpies are intermediaries between mortal men and spirits. I couldn't pronounce a lot of the place names. How do Scots say 'Auchterarder'?

The sharp and rugged Cuillin mountains on the Isle of Skye beckoned to me. Tartans, blared colour from thousands of pages. Histories of clan wars – whew! I read until my eyes bleared over. I wanted to smell the air of this romantic and ancient land. I wanted to eat what they ate. My mother's copy of Walter Scott's poetry became a handy reference. His description of the Highlands beguiled me to the point when I wanted to tramp the 'wild and strange retreat' as he had done.

I googled the village of Glenhill.

> Population: 1200
> Main Industries: Farming and engineering
> Churches: 2 – St Conval's and Presbyterian
> Schools: Primary: 1 Catholic 1 Protestant
> Post Offices: 1
> Chemist:1
> Health Centre: Next town Paisley
> Doctor: None (see above)

I tried to envisage what Claire and my grandparents looked like. I asked the walls questions: did the McCrae's get together often? Andy and Jack were older than my mother. Were they grey-haired? Bald? I felt something start within me. Slowly, it overcame resistance to a weight embedded in my heart.

I didn't know what to say to my grandparents so I scribbled a one-page note and enclosed my Ordinary Degree grad photo and some of Mum while she still looked well. Fate seemed to be working out a new chapter in my life. I knew I'd done the right thing when I got Claire's next message:

Hello Anna

Grandpa says to thank you for sending the photos. He's put your graduation picture and your ma's in real swanky frames. They now sit in the centre of the mantelpiece in the living room. He says to everyone who comes in, 'That's oor Eleanor, and her lassie, Anna.' I think he and Gran would like it if we all bowed as if it was some kind of shrine. Grandma reaches up and touches your faces and cries. She had a stroke last year that affected her speech and she drags her left leg a bit.

Cheerio for now – Claire

**21**

I filled my days cycling, walking, re-organising things around home and hoping for news about my future. Mardi and Augie were regular visitors. When Joe was home, he and I would spend time together and sometimes the four of us would team up for a meal or a movie.

Joe sat with me when I Googled Scotland. Sometimes he'd research geological sites and sometimes we'd check out accommodation and transport around places we'd found.

He'd say something like 'Look, Anna, y'see these mountains? Dalradian 610 million years old.'

'Wonder what it'd be like to climb to the top. Bet the view would take your breath away.'

'Sheeesh! You'd have no fuckin' breath left after a climb like that.'

And so descriptions of rock formations got entangled in my oooohs and aaaahs at the sight of the colours on the slopes of the ancient majestic peaks. And we'd end up in each other's arms laughing and breathless.

Joe bought a book on Scottish expressions with a glossary of dialectic words. Sometimes when he and Mardi were around, we'd open a bottle of wine and have some fun with the meaning and pronunciation of words like bairrrrn, cannae, willnae, shouldnae. We rolled Rs until our tongues were sore, and practised saying 'loch' and 'Lochaber' from the back of our throats. By the time we'd run out of wine, our jaws would be aching from laughing. Augie opted out of the exercise and played moderator.

One night Joe gave us song sheets with the words of Scottish ditties he'd downloaded from the internet, without tunes. So we sang about braes and bonnie lassies to tunes of Australian songs like 'The Road to Gundagai'.

**22**

The day my uni results arrived, Mardi called in and within half an hour Joe and Augie pranced up the driveway. Augie carried a brown paper wrapped bottle in each hand and Joe had two family-sized pizza boxes. He threw them onto the table and danced me around the kitchen chanting, 'I knew you could do it… I knew you could do it' and Mardi and Augie joined the chorus.

'Top fuckin' mark for the course,' Joe shouted while opening a bottle of Moët to toast my success.

'Well, you three deserve some of the credit. You've encouraged me along the way,' I said, looking at three smiling faces.

'What d'you mean? We were the ones out partying. You spent your time poring over books and thumping away on your keyboard. The credit's all yours, m'dear,' Joe said, grinning and refilling our glasses.

'What's next?' Mardi asked. 'Scotland?'

'Don't know yet.'

'When will you know?' Augie asked.

'Soon, as I hear about the course at London Uni.' I put the kettle on for coffee.

Joe, engrossed in reading my final essay, said nothing.

# 23

Christmas shopping in the city and my feet were on fire from pounding concrete. I found a soft seat in a corner of Hudson's coffee shop and decided to check the mail I'd picked up on my way out. A Christmas card from Lettie. A letter from uni: 'Congratulations: Outstanding results. European Prize.' A second letter with the uni logo fell from the pile. It was confirmation of acceptance and scholarship approval for the course I'd applied for at London Uni. I threw the letters on the table and gasped a loud 'YES!' People at the next table looked at me like they thought I was some crazy person. My hands shook. I could hardly tear the tube of sugar open and when I tried to pour it into my coffee it scattered, like tiny shiny fragments of quartz, over the mail I'd just been reading.

Stop. Gather your wits.

Like a fast-flowing river, so many strings of my destiny were being pulled towards something unseen. I wondered if ever they'd be woven into a cohesive pattern. I nearly left my parcels behind in the excitement of the moment.

Getting my passport, arranging flights, making decisions about what clothes (must buy a lightweight raincoat) and books to take (would the uni library have what I need?) kept me going at full speed and took up my time over the next weeks.

The night before I left Adelaide I drove up to Windy Point lookout where Mum and Dad used to take me on summer evenings. It looked as though a glittering necklace snaked around the bends and curves of the Adelaide hills until it got lost amongst the yellow lights of main city roads. While watching those amber tracks, I wondered what paths I'd tread in the coming year and where they might lead me. The wind bullied my hair into a frantic farce of style until rain flattened it into submission.

## 24

I am writing this at Heathrow Airport, the centre of the world. While waiting for my flight to Glasgow, I ingest the sounds and sights of the terminal. Fuzziness in my ears from the descent helps to blanket the constant warnings about unattended baggage blaring from ubiquitous black boxes.

People are rushing. Walking. Waiting. Africans in bright togas and turbans. Indians in saris. Scots in kilts. A Texan or two. In the corner on a wooden bench are three women dressed in full, black chadors. Only eyes like jet beads and an occasional movement under the fabric establish life beneath the folds. An old man with a pock-marked face is standing in front of them holding a bunch of documents that look like passports and boarding passes. How do the women breathe? Do they ever feel the sun on their skin? A group with Deutsch Travelland name tags and bags are discussing the inconvenience of a delay in the flight in loud guttural voices. They stick so close to their luggage it looks like they are glued together.

The mass of humanity moving around me is less impressive than the thought that I now stand a short distance from the roads where Cromwell's armies marched and the place where the first Charles lost his head. I pondered the consequences that civil wars and the search for religious freedom had had on this land. And how the leaving of Britain in more recent migrations affected people like my parents. Eventually and somehow, a state of order emerges from this bedlam to propel passengers to their destinations. Amazing.

**25**

Minutes after hearing my flight called, I walked from the terminal through a connecting tunnel into the Caledonian Airlines plane. Although Mum's Scottish accent had been modified by time and Australian expressions, the soft accents of the flight attendants reminded me of her voice. I smiled when I saw the short kilty uniforms and tilted tammies they wore. Suddenly, I'm in Scotland. It was like being a character in a fantasy adventure – like the children in the C.S. Lewis story, going from England to Narnia through a wardrobe. Mum used to read me to sleep with that one.

I had two weeks before my course started. Enough time to meet the McCraes of Glenhill and connect with my mother's past. The tension in my body could've been excitement, apprehension or fatigue.

I leafed through a magazine then fiddled with the audio system on my seat. By the time I'd found a station that I liked, and eaten lunch, we'd landed. A maze of yellow lines on a blue carpet led me to the arrival hall.

Through a glass partition, beyond the bumping, pushing people around the luggage carousel, I saw a middle-aged man waving a white piece of cardboard with 'Anna Banfield' scrawled on it. I waved to him. He grinned and waved back.

He had a stocky build, and a thick thatch of white hair. His complexion looked like he'd spend a lot of time outdoors but the contradiction of dark suit and tie gave me the impression he'd just come from a business meeting. His smile reminded me of Mum. I liked his face. Thinking I'd see someone that could be Claire, I looked at the people standing around him but he seemed to be on his own. Every few minutes while waiting for my bags to come along the conveyor belt I'd look out to him and we'd wave to each other. At last a trolley suitcase, and an oversized backpack with gaudy pink ribbons tied on the handles, appeared through a space in the wall. A young man standing beside me saw me reaching for them. He smiled at me and hauled my luggage to a clear space. A few steps through the automatic glass doors and I was face to face with the first of the McCraes.

'Hello, Anna, grrrreat to see ye,' he said, 'I'm Andy,' and his smile spread over me like a warm blanket. His voice was warm – like ochre. When he took my hands in his, they disappeared as if they were the hands of a small child. He held me close then stepped back. He studied every feature of my face and hugged me again. I thought I could smell the sea. He looked at my hair and said, 'I expected your hair tae be auburn like Eleanor's.'

I felt choked – unable to say a word.

We stood smiling at each other until a voice called above the transient sounds around us, 'Dad! Anna! Anna!'

I turned towards the sound. A woman weaving through trolleys and groups of people hurried towards us.

'It's Claire. She's aye late.' Andy raised his hand and waved to her.

I nearly fainted. The woman rushing to my side looked like a young version of my mother. Claire wore a loose, white linen sleeveless dress that stopped just above her knees and showed off her sun-tanned arms and legs. She had a neat slim build and stood above me by about four centimetres. I was thunderstruck when I noticed her hair. Thick panels of shiny auburn fell over her shoulders – exactly like Mum's used to be. Claire wore no jewellery or make-up and her face was free of lines or blemishes. Her nails were white, tapering and polished like ivory. Her hands were long and thin like Mum's had been and the only thing she carried was her car keys. For a split second, an image of Mum running on the beach, flashed in my mind. I didn't know what Claire did for a living but I thought she would be a great subject for an ad in health magazines.

'So sorry I'm late,' she gasped with no sign of a Scottish accent.

'Accident on the freeway. Got held up for ages.' Then she took one of my hands in both of hers and said, 'It's so good to meet you at last, Anna. How are you?'

All I could manage as a response was a quiet 'Hi.'

I stood and stared at her. She met my gaze openly, with candour.

Andy broke the suspense by grabbing the handle of my case, picking up my backpack and ushering us towards the exit. The first thing I noticed when we got outside was the softness of the breeze. It was just enough to cool my head without making me shiver with cold. A light mist blurred the outlines of cars and buildings like an Impressionist painting. Stepping into the cool air made me think of early autumn mornings in Adelaide.

**26**

The hills beyond the airport looked like great mounds of blue-black earth. The next thing I noticed was the strident, clear sounds of Scottish voices, booming across the tarmac of the parking lot. The speakers seemed to want the world to hear their opinions on airline food, and about the bargains they'd picked up in Cyprus or Spain.

Andy loaded my luggage into the boot of his car and said that I should go with Claire in her car. 'It'll give baith o' you a chance to get acquainted. I'll look after this lot.'

'Thanks, Dad,' Claire said. 'I'm parked miles away, Anna. Hope you don't mind the walk.'

'It is so good to be out in the air. I think I could run for miles.' I matched her pace.

When we were settled in the car, I said she looked like Mum.

She smiled and said, 'I don't mind that one tiny bit. From what I've heard, she was beautiful.'

'Who did you hear that from?'

'When we got your first email, I heard Grandpa and Dad talk about "oor Eleanor" and how much I looked like her. I felt flattered.'

Claire's voice was different from Mum's – not as soft, and I was glad for that. For the first few minutes on the way to Andy's house, she bashed my ears with questions. 'How was Singapore? Are you hungry? This your first overseas trip? How long've you got in Scotland?' The speed of delivery gave me little opportunity to answer – and it reminded me of the way Mardi prattled on at times. Then she said, 'The old folk are so excited about meeting you, Anna. We managed to get Grandma a wheelchair for the day. Since she had the stroke she gets really tired. A taxi picks her up three times a week and takes her to therapy at the local health centre and she's improved out of sight from how she was six months ago.'

I was about to ask Claire about herself, what she did for a living and about her social life, when she pulled into a driveway and said, 'We're here.'

**27**

The hullabaloo that hit me when the front door opened made me want to turn the volume down. Claire ushered me in. Andy called attention.

'Quiet, everrrryone! Meet your Australian cousin, Anna.'

Eyes from every corner of the room watched me and I hoped I didn't look as tired as I felt.

Two women stopped fussing with food to reach out hands of welcome saying, 'Hello, Anna. How are you?'

They were Claire's older sisters, Ellen and Molly. Chairs lined each side of a table laden with plates of sandwiches, cakes and pastries. I saw some children fidgeting and giggling in one corner and a group of teenagers in another. The teenagers wore short black leather skirts teamed with gaudy prints and knee-high boots. With mobile phones at their ears, they would've fitted easily into a scene in Rundle Mall.

I spotted Grandpa right away. He was the only elderly man in the company. As he came towards me, he limped a bit and leaned to one side. He held a walking stick in one hand and a baseball cap in the other. You could see where the hat had flattened his white hair against his head. He had a slim build and his lean, tight face looked like it had been scrubbed clean and dipped in sunshine. His eyes, blue and sparkling like polished metal, glinted behind frameless glasses. Creases down the front of his trousers looked like they could cut butter, and his shoes shone like patent leather.

When he got close to me, he put his walking stick against the wall, his hat on a little table and said, 'Hello, hen.' The soft greeting had trouble leaving his lips as he took both my hands in his and kissed my brow.

I hugged him, saying, 'Hello, Grandpa,' forcing the lump in my throat back to where it had come from.

Grandma sat in a wheelchair by a window looking at me. I'd never met anyone who'd had a stroke before and I was surprised at how well she looked. She wasn't scrawny like some old people I'd seen back home. When I looked at her face, I could see where Mum's gorgeous complexion had come from. It was almost transparent alabaster. Except for a few tiny blue veins at each temple, her skin looked like it had been polished with cream. I walked across to her side.

Big, fat, wet, tears, rolled down her cheeks and she said something like 'Huh…wo,' grasped my hand and held it tight.

I looked into her eyes and we stayed locked to each other, and still. Then I bent down to be closer to her and said, 'Hello, Grandma' and gave her a peck on the cheek. I couldn't think of anything else to say.

She sighed and said 'Hu…wo' again and shook her head like a puppy bothered by a horsefly, before letting my hand drop.

Most of Grandma's hair was white. Little streaks of dark like thin pencil lines on an old jotter filtered through it, as if they'd forgotten to change colour. It was swept up off her neck and brow and piled up in a knot on top of her head with wide combs at each side holding it in place. Hints of eyeshadow around her eyes accented hazel irises. She sat straight, as if a steel bar was pinned to her spine. One arm lay listless on her lap and her long slim fingers, just like Mum's, looked as frail as honey-eater bones. She wore a bottle-green linen dress with a white collar. She looked beautiful. Someone brought us each a cup of tea and a plate with a pastry on it.

A boy about eight introduced himself as Gerard. His hair reminded me of a summer sun set at Henley Beach. He pointed to a red-headed doll whose smile showed a gap where her two front teeth should've been.

'She's my sister Sheena, and she wants to hear you say something Australian, and she wants to know if you have kangaroos in your back garden.'

'Well, Gerard, tell Sheena that when I say "G'day" it's the same as your "Hello" and when I say "See you later" it's like your "Cheerio". And tell her no, we don't have kangaroos in our garden, we go to a place called Cleland Wildlife Park to see them.'

'Thanks. See you later,' he quipped, and moved to join his sister and cousins.

I could see him whispering to them while they looked over at me and giggled.

Later, the young people bombarded me with questions about Australia:

'What's it like to have Christmas in the sunshine?'

'Do you have roast turkey or just cold stuff?'

'Do children wear school uniforms?'

'How hot does it get in summer?'

'How many people get killed by sharks?'

Older people wanted to know about the kind of life Mum and Dad had built. They asked about real estate prices, employment statistics, the climate, and government policies on things like refugees and the environment.

Such a celebration. I felt like royalty. I must have had fifteen cups of tea and enough pastries and cakes to last me for six months. I thought if Joe were here, he'd be lapping up the food and reaching out for more. I'd never seen so many people in one house. As they milled around talking over and above each other, I had to concentrate hard to make some sense of the hubbub.

I jumped between conversations as if I was constantly changing radio stations. I felt dizzy and disorientated. My ears buzzed with voices talking about things I couldn't understand no matter how hard I concentrated.

By early evening my grandparents had grown tired and everyone started to leave. Some shuffled around searching under chairs and tables for bags. Others carried crumby platters, high above the heads of children. I could hear the clatter of dishes and voices chatting while they cleaned up in the kitchen. People bumped into each other as the last remnants of food were cleared from the table. Children reclaimed Gameboys and Yu-Gi-Oh cards from reluctant borrowers.

Claire helped my grandparents out to Andy's car and told me she'd see me next day.

<h1 style="text-align:center">28</h1>

Although it was midsummer, my grandparents' house was cool and Andy turned on a gas heater with fake flames that darted around fake coal. He put my luggage in one of the bedrooms and made us a cup of tea before saying goodnight. Grandpa had trouble manoeuvring the wheelchair through the doors of the living room, but he wouldn't accept my offer of help.

In spite of the span of time, I felt that the threads of his life and mine were entwined around love for my mother. When Andy had gone, we settled down in the living room. Grandma tried to say something. I couldn't make any sense of it but Grandpa got up and brought a walking frame to her. He flipped the footrests of the wheelchair up and waited close by while she struggled to her feet. He took her damaged arm and placed her hand on one of the handgrips of the walker. She followed with the other. In spite of the weakness in her leg, she moved easily across the room.

She stood in front of the mantelpiece and pointed to my photo. 'Thank you,' she said clearly, then pointed to one beside it with Mum in it and looked straight into my eyes. She started to say something with an 'eh' sound but couldn't get her tongue around whatever the word was.

'She's tryin' tae say Ellie's name. She's been tryin' for weeks now, but hasn't managed it yet,' Grandpa piped up, 'but she's determined, an' I'm sure she will one o' these days.'

He picked up an old cardigan from the back of a chair and put it on then slipped his shoes off and put on a pair of slippers that looked like they'd been around for a while. He leaned back in his chair and said, 'that's much better. These days I like tae be comfortable.'

Grandma trundled her frame back to a chair by the fireside.

'Y'know, Grandpa, Mum and Dad had a good life together. I overheard her saying one time that leaving Scotland was the best outcome for everyone. When I butted in and asked her why? She just went all vague on me.'

Grandma started waving her good arm and shaking her head. 'No! No!' Her tongue got tied around the next few sounds but I gathered the sense of it was that it was not a good thing for Grandma that Mum had left.

Being with my grandparents in the house my mother had left as a young girl, and watching their faces, I wanted to believe they'd treated her memory with honour. I wanted to ask Grandma what had happened between her and Mum, but decided to wait until Grandpa and I were alone. Instead, I asked him where he kept drinking glasses. He pointed to a cabinet in the corner and I poured him a shot of single malt from a bottle of Macallan 12 I'd bought at the duty-free shop.

When I offered a drink to Gran, she shook her head signalling 'No.'

'How did ye know this is my favourite?' Grandpa asked as I handed it to him.

'Pure guesswork,' I said.

I kept looking at Grandma, trying to find flashes of Mum's features in the tilt of her head, the shape of her mouth, the size of her hands and fingers, but nothing in my memory connected them to each other. When I bent to give her a hug, she grasped my arms and murmured something into my jacket. I looked into eyes that stayed still and impenetrable.

'I didn't hear, can you tell me again?'

'Don' liiiiik isky. Liiiik tea.'

'Will I get you a cup of tea now?'

'No o o, laaadr.' She sat back in her chair and closed her eyes.

## 29

It was still light outside and when Grandpa finished his drink I asked him to show me around the garden. Clumps of rhubarb and pots of parsley grew in a corner beside the shed (he called it 'the hut'). The vegetable patch had lots of green tops sticking up from soil that looked almost black. A newspaper lay on a wooden bench and the air smelled of roses.

In the silence that lay between us I had the feeling that Grandpa wanted to say something. I asked him about the last time he'd seen Mum.

'Come an' sit down for a wee while,' he said, taking my arm towards the bench. 'I'm no' sure how much ye know about what happened to your mother, Anna, and I don't want tae talk about it right now. All I can say at this point is that she brought your father here hopin' the quarrel wi' your grandma could be sorted out. It fairly broke my heart tae hear the things they said tae each other that day. Ellie was in tears when she left. I never thought for a minute I wouldn't ever see her again. If I'd known that, I would've begged your grandma on my knees tae think again about makin' peace wi' her. I wanted them tae sit down around the table. All the worries in the world can be discussed ower a pot o' tea. Maybe no' resolved, but at least a civilised discussion is better than a' that spleen gettin' spilled without thinkin'.'

'Do you remember what Dad said?' I asked.

'Well, no' exactly, the man was in a quandary, so sensible about the situation. He only wanted peace between them. Your dad an' I would've been good friends if we'd had the chance. I liked him.' Grandpa spoke into the gloaming with a slow patient weariness. He told me about a time when Mum had gone off alone on a new bike he'd bought her. She'd been away for hours, and they were about to launch a search party when she appeared walking and pushing the bike along beside her. The chain had broken and she'd had to walk nearly five miles home. (I had to remind myself that this was in the days before mobile phones.)

'Your mam was a devil for adventure. Right frae her youngest years, she had tae explore beyond oor patch o' earth. I think she was born wi' the wanderlust.'

I listened carefully, letting the warm sound of his voice and the words roll out around me. And I noticed that the deeper he went into his soul, the more Scottish his words became. It seemed to me that only the ancient dialect would suit the emotions of the moment.

I heard someone tapping on the kitchen window and looked around to see Gran. I couldn't hear what she was trying to say, but it looked to me like she was scooping up handfuls of air and throwing it over her shoulder.

'That's the signal for us tae come inside. It's time for a bit o' supper,' Grandpa said, standing up and waving to Gran. 'We'll talk more when your gran has gone tae bed.'

We were about to move inside when a voice called out from the front gate, 'Yoo hoo… Is that Ellie's lass?'

'It's Fiona,' Grandpa said. 'She's been desperate tae meet you.' He raised his voice, 'I'll see ye later, Fiona…must go an' atten' tae the boss.' He went inside.

## 30

Fiona wore a calf-length navy skirt and matching jacket with a white blouse. She seemed loaded down with a briefcase and laptop computer and I could see a mobile phone on the side of a leather shoulder bag that slid off her shoulder as she trudged up the pathway. She had a plump figure and her greying hair straggled around her face.

She talked as she walked towards me. 'Sorry I couldn't get here sooner. I've been at a conference for the past three days.' She plonked her bags on the pathway, smiled at me and offered her hand. 'Welcome tae Scotland, Anna. Since I heard you were comin' home, I've been so excited. I was so sorry tae hear about your mam.'

Before I had time to respond to that, she said, 'You look like your father.'

'Do you remember him?' I asked.

'Remember? How could I forget such a handsome man. He was gorgeous.'

We laughed together the way friends do when they share a common bond.

'How long will you be staying in Scotland?'

'Well, I have to be in London by the last week of July.'

'That's grand,' she said. 'Hope you'll have a few hours tae spare. You an' I have a lot o' talkin' to do. Must go. The grandchildren need attention.'

We promised to meet next afternoon and she bustled off to attend to small children calling to her from across the oval.

# 31

I was sitting with my grandparents in the living room once again. They both seemed deep in thought. Grandma's head lolled to one side and she looked almost asleep.

Grandpa turned to me and said, 'I feel vexed for your gran, Anna.' He looked over at Grandma who sat slouched in her wheelchair plucking at the shawl that covered her knees. 'Times like this she loses contact so right now the pleasure of getting to know you is lost tae her.' He tottered over to me, took both my hands in his and looked into my face. 'I'm happy tae get the chance tae welcome ye intae ma hame.'

He nodded towards Grandma. 'I think the excitement o' so many people aroun' the day has tired her oot, but she'll be better after a good night's sleep.'

Then he leant over her, the light from the fire picking out the silver in his hair and the ruddy tones of his outdoor complexion. 'This is Anna, oor Eleanor's lassie from Australia,' he shouted into her ear. 'D'ye remember Ellie?'

Grandma just stared ahead.

He took the cup from her and turned to me. 'Sometimes she seems no' tae hear. The pleasure of enjoyin' your mother's company is lost tae her. But I know she regrets how she treated Ellie an' I'm glad that she's met you. C'mon, Cissie, it's time for bed.' He shook her gently then helped her to her feet.

That was the first time I'd heard my grandmother's name. I stood up to hug her and said, 'It's great to see you and great to be here. Goodnight, Gran.'

She grasped my arms and then took one of my hands, kissed it, and trundled off to her room with Grandpa tottering behind her.

When he came back by the fireside, I asked him, 'Is Gran's condition getting better?'

'Oh my, yes,' he said. 'She could hardly walk a few months ago and now she manages fine wi' a frame. Now, Anna, I'm anxious tae talk about Ellie, but if you're too tired frae the journey, it can wait till mornin'.'

'No, that's fine, Grandpa. I'm okay.'

'Y'ken, Anna, she wis jist a slip o' a girl, only sixteen…hidnae yet learned the ways o' the world an' it seems tae me she made a bad choice goin' oot wi' that lout.'

Red fake sparks spurted from fake black coal like the anger spewing from some dark part of him.

'I should've stood up tae yer grandma. She wiz too hard on yer mither. Noo look at her.'

A feeling like an arc of electric current shot through me. 'What d'you mean? Who did she go out with?'

'Dae ye mean tae tell me, Anna, that you don't know about why Ellie left us?'

'Nope. I only know that something bad happed to her, but the details – no idea.' I waited.

His body slackened. He gulped some air through his mouth and stared at me. 'Y'see, Anna, your gran wanted Ellie tae go oot wi Frank Welsh, a Catholic boy. She did. Only tae pacify her mother. But he turned out tae be a real bad egg. Then Peter came intae her life an' that was that. Ellie never told a soul about what happened. She left the village. Anyway, Anna, the details o' that time are a' in the past. It's no' somethin' I'll discuss with you. One thing that pleases me,' Grandpa went on, 'she kept our photos an' you're here now. That tells me she never forgot us.'

Listening to him talk about Mum like this brought the anger I'd felt towards her rising to my throat. Why hadn't she written to her dad, or to one of her brothers?

'It's getting' late. So I'm off tae bed now, and I'll sleep well knowin' you're in the house. Our heads'll be clearer in the mornin' and we'll talk more then. Claire has left towels an' things in your mother's old room for you, but if there's anythin' else you need, just let me know. It's the last door on the left doon the lobby. Goodnight, Anna.' He patted me on the back, and shuffled off.

I heard their bedroom door close and went outside to stand in the gloaming, amazed that at ten-thirty at night, it was not yet dark. Fragrance from flowers around me reminded me of our garden at home. The colours and scents were similar. Being here, in her father's garden, I wanted to shake Mum back to me. I wanted to see her standing beside me, telling me about her young days. And I wanted to see her sitting with her parents, listening to them laugh and reminiscing together the way it was with the three of us when Dad was still around.

I stared so long at the bushes and trees that they began to take on the shape and size of my mother. In spite of the still-warm air, I shivered.

**32**

The worst thing about my mother dying was watching her healthy skin fade to a yellowy grey colour and seeing the bones shine through like white sticks under her eyes and around her jaw-line. She had beautiful hair once. Thick, auburn – the kind you see in ads for shampoo. She used to spend hours brushing it until it gleamed. At the end, all that remained were a few sparse strands of white hair plastered to her skull.

When I'd watched strangers wash her hidden parts, or stick needles into her and probe her form, I wanted to pull them away from her.

Once, I yelled at a nurse, 'Leave my mother alone, you stupid bitch!'

'So sorry, Anna, but she needs to be turned.' Then she said, 'You can help me if you want to.'

I slunk into a chair in the corner and hid my eyes from her compassion.

I loathed the indignities of Mum's dying days. The smells from her body, slowly decomposing from within, assaulted my senses. I felt torn between wanting to move away and wanting to linger beside her. I remember stroking her arms and hands. Her skin was dry. Hot. Rough. And when I bent towards her to kiss the arthritic knobs on each of her fingers, I remembered how these hands had stroked my back at times when I'd been bent over books for hours. And I remembered how they'd planted and pruned to create the best-looking garden in our neighbourhood.

The injustices of her suffering battered my heart. During those last days, only the beep and lights of the monitor by her bedside told me she was still alive – until the pinpoints of light that were her eyes faded with her last breath.

# 33

Everything in my grandparents' house had a taint of decay underlying a faint whiff of something like White King. It was as if someone had tried to cover up mould in the aged carpets and cupboards.

Statues of saints and pictures of the Sacred Heart and the Virgin Mary dominated every room. Mum's room had a picture above the bed of the Pope adorned with a rosary. The only sound was the tick tick of a clock on the mantelpiece above an empty grate in the fireplace. Two long small-paned windows almost filled the wall that faced the door. A carpet covered the floor from the edge of the bed to the skirting board of the window wall and I could see faint traces of pink roses and green leaves in the pattern around the edges. The centre had faded to grey with time and treading feet. Sadness seemed to crouch in the corners and I wished I had an antidote to counter it.

When I opened the wardrobe door to hang up my jacket, I jumped at the squeaking sound – as if some tiny creature was caught in the wooden joints. I tried to find the scent of her amongst the furniture and in the bedclothes but only the scent of old sweat and stale perfume oozed out from a couple of dresses and shirts dangling from wire coat hangers.

As I crept into bed that first night, I tried to conjure Mum's young face. But I could only see the shape of her, huddled in a hospital bed like a bag of old clothes waiting for disposal. And a dim yellow light gave an eerie colour to the walls and to her face. Her bony hands clutched the edge of a silk nightie that I'd brought for her. She'd loved silk next to her skin and would often spend her whole clothes allowance on expensive lingerie

I dreamt.

I'm in the basement of some tall building. Tangled metal pipes surround me and impede my struggles to get to a rusty, twisted staircase I could see in the distance. It feels like I'm starting a journey of some kind with no clear destination. I reach the bottom step and start to climb towards a light that shines through gaps in a glass roof above me. Sometimes I slip back to where I'd come from. I am exhausted and my hands are sore. Suddenly, I look up to a sky as blue as the summer sky like you see in the Australian desert and I'm sitting in lush green grass with my mother behind me braiding my hair. She doesn't speak. I think, close your eyes, Anna. Reach out your hand. Touch her.

I woke up with a terrible fear that my mother was dying. Then I looked around and saw the daggy drapes and old carpet. My fear changed to a loneliness that spread through my veins and bones to my fingers and toes where it lay for a long, long time.

**34**

Next morning I lay in bed until I heard subdued noises in the hallway. Doors opening and closing and the sound of running water signalled my grandparents were starting their routine.

I wandered outside to take a look at the day. I gazed across rooftops to the hills and let the soft gentle sun warm my shoulders. I could hear an occasional bark from a distant dog and see a woman in the garden next door hanging sheets on the washing line.

Grandpa appeared at my side wearing the Akubra I'd brought for him. 'G'day,' he said.

'Hello,' I answered.

We sniggered.

He pointed to some plants growing in neat rows. 'Can ye tell me what they might be?'

'Well, I think that's carrots and behind that is spinach and those on the trellis look like climbing beans.'

'No' bad for an Aussie. I'm impressed. Your mother's taught ye well. Did she ever talk aboot the times she an' I spent in the garden?'

'Well, she didn't so much talk about it, Grandpa, but our garden has many similar plants to yours. She planted a rosemary hedge along the driveway, and clumps of bluebells, that burst into life each spring along the fence line, just like you have here. So I'm sure she thought about you.'

He moved towards the house. 'Grandma's waitin' on her breakfast. We better go in.'

Grandma was leaning over the sink trying to fill the kettle. She wore a bright loose-fitting floral dress with buttons down the front. Her hair was held back from her face with side combs then hung free to her shoulders. I took the kettle from her. She turned to me, smiled and tried to say something. She shrugged in frustration and nudged her frame around to a chair at the end of the table.

While Grandpa showed me where the tea things and cereals were kept, I set the table. He tucked a napkin into Grandma's collar and moved the walking frame into a corner.

'Who were the teenagers at Andy's place yesterday?' I asked him.

'Aw, they're Andy's grand-weans and their pals. To tell ye the truth, Anna, I don't know some o' their names.'

'Well, there's no' much hope o' me knowin' them, eh?'

He chortled at my poor attempt at the local vernacular, and Grandma gave me a one-hand clap on the table. I toasted bread and made a pot of tea, while he gave me the run-down on family:

'Claire's the youngest of Andy's three daughters and you'll meet Jack's three sons at the party on the weekend. Gerard and Sheena are Jack's grandchildren.'

Amongst all this family I still couldn't shake the feeling of loss. The need to resolve the gaps in my mother's past gnawed at my conscience.

As if he knew where my thoughts were, Grandpa said, 'Y'ken, Anna, it was as if oor Eleanor had walked through a door and locked it tight against any interference or contact from the life she'd known. When I got Kate's letter saying they'd left Oban, it very near sent me to my grave. They didnae even bother to tell Kate they were going to Australia. I guess they didn't want to burden her wi' knowledge that would cause her to worry about whether to tell us or no'. Why d'ye think she never wrote to us?'

'Don't know, Grandpa. I've been trying to work that out – I wish she had, but I do know that she was looking forward to coming back to Scotland for a holiday.'

Grandpa and I took our mugs of tea out to the garden and sat on the bench.

He pulled his hat over his face and lay back with his hands lying lightly on his stomach. 'Did she ever talk to ye about us?' he asked.

'I know you taught Mum a lot about gardening,' I said. 'She loved to grow things and I'd heard her say to Dad that the smell of newly turned earth reminded her of you.'

Grandpa lifted his hat from his face and looked at me, grinning. 'I'm so glad that stayed wi' Ellie – I used tae get her to pick a handful o' soil and smell the freshness o' it.' When he said this, the smile on his face made tracks from his mouth to his eyes. He put his hat back over his face. 'What can ye tell me about them goin' tae Australia, Anna?'

'I know they were married in a registry office in Southampton. I know that next day they sailed on the *Castel Felice* for Australia. I don't know why they made that decision. Mum talked a lot about the voyage and the excitement of sailing through the Suez Canal. When they were docked at Aden for a little while, they watched native boys dive from little boats to catch coins that passengers threw from the ship. I know they celebrated Mum's seventeenth birthday the day the ship crossed the Equator, so she had two birthdays that year. Dad used to tease her about being a year older than she admitted to, and only two years younger than him, not three, like shown on their passports.'

Grandpa said quietly from under his hat, 'So they must have left Oban soon after they came here that day. D'ye know, Anna, my sister Kate had been a great source of comfort tae Ellie. They left instructions wi' a florist in the town to send their thanks wi' a bouquet.'

'What did Kate have to say about that?'

'Well, a' she said was that she wished them a life o' peace and happiness – whatever form that took. Kate and Cissie never got on, y'know.'

He said nothing for a while. I thought he'd dozed off.

Then, a whisper from under the brim of his hat. 'Tell me about when she got sick. I'd like tae know about that.'

I started to tell him about the time Mum had collapsed in the garden but only got as far watching her plant the bulbs. 'I'll tell you more in a minute. I've got something for you.'

## 35

I raced into my room, rummaged through my flight bag and found Mum's diary. I put her letter to me in a side pocket of my bag and returned to the kitchen. Grandma was sitting at the kitchen table massaging her limp arm with her good hand. I called Grandpa inside and made another pot of tea.

I unwound the scarf from the diary and put it around Grandma's shoulders. 'This is from Mum. And this is what she wrote before she died,' I said, giving her the diary. 'I'd like you to have it.'

She clenched the diary in her good hand and crushed it to her breast. As soon as I released it, I wanted it back. The way you sometimes buy a gift for a friend, but want to keep it for yourself. A fleeting thought about Mum's honest words made me wonder if I'd done the right thing by giving the book to Gran.

Grandma tried to say something. She clenched her good fist, shook it in frustration, and then pressed fingers into the middle of her brow as if she was squeezing the words out of her muddled mind. Grandpa failed to make words out of the sounds.

She said over and over something like 'Noa...uv...er' then she'd take a deep breath and try again, 'Noa...uv...er.' She looked at me with an intensity that scorched my heart.

I got a notebook and pen and asked her to write it down.

'NO!' She shouted, and slapped the table. She picked up the ends of the scarf with two shaking fingers and touched it to her face with slow soft strokes, her eyes shut tight, and lips pursed as if she was afraid to let her heartache show.

Grandpa said, 'She's been forcing hersel' tae say as much as she can. She feels that if she keeps writin' things down, it'll hold her back frae speakin' right. The truth o' the matter is, Anna, Cissie's doctor says that writing for stroke patients is nigh impossible ''cos they cannae find the words in the first place. Her speech will come back afore the ability to write.'

I slid the notebook and pen into my jacket pocket, then stood behind her. I massaged her shoulders and neck for a little while, then left them with the excuse that I'd to finish unpacking. Seeing this old pair shuffling through their life, I believed that Mum 'learning not to hate' her mother was not enough of a resolution.

<h1 style="text-align:center">36</h1>

The sun streamed into the room, and through the windows I could see silver ribbons of water dividing the faraway hills into sections like a giant cake. Mum had told me once that when she was a little girl, and the sun peeked through the rain in places, she'd look to these landmarks and see rainbows, and she'd give them special names – like Fiona, Anne Marie, Kathleen. I stood where she might have stood and stared through my tears at swaying lines of silver. The thought came to me then that my grandparents had missed some of the best years of my mother's life and I'd had them all.

I tried to see Mum in her shirt-waister with a red belt nipping her waist and perhaps a ponytail and poppet beads and stiletto-heeled shoes. And she'd be posing in this very mirror turning her head this way, then that way, pouting her lips. Where was her collection of Galliards folk records she'd told me about? And the Beatles and Beach Boys? And Elvis? And did she dance around on this carpet I'm standing on now? She was so totally non-existent in this room.

I tidied up my bags quickly and joined my grandparents in the kitchen for lunch.

While we ate, Grandpa said, 'I couldnae believe Ellie would leave and never come back. I kept hopin' that one day I'd look up from weedin' carrots or prunin' the roses an' she'd walk through the gate. I just wish I could bring her back tae the time when bruises could be kissed away. I was so wrong about things.' The regret in his voice oozed over the chair he sat on, spread through the room and over the walls and floor like oil from a damaged container.

I rose from the table and put my arms around him.

## 37

Claire arrived and suggested we take a walk around Glenhill while our grandparents went to their room for a nap. I wanted Mardi to know I'd arrived safely, so I popped into the local library to check my email.

Mardi's message was all about rotten weather and long working hours. 'Missing you' was tagged on to the end of her complaints.

From Joe, 'Missing you.'

I replied, 'Et tu.'

'My laptop's available anytime you want,' Claire said.

'No worries, Claire. Haven't unpacked mine yet, but the library's handy for now.'

We walked past the building where Mum had gone to school – now a depot for heavy transport. The sheds where children had sheltered from the rain were filled with crates and cartons and wheelie bins.

As we strolled along, Claire told me about the plans for Grandpa's birthday party. 'We're getting caterers in and we've organised a ceilidh band for the dancing.'

'Sounds like it'll be good fun.' I said.

'Yup. And being in a church hall on a Saturday night'll be a change for the young folk of the family.'

'How often do you go to church, Claire?'

'Only sometimes. Depends. Maybe midnight Mass at Christmas, or on Easter Sunday morning. It's not really my thing. Dad and Jack stopped going years ago – something to do with the feud between your mother and Grandma. I think the next generation never found the habit.' As she spoke, she flicked back her long hair the way Mum used to do.

'Do you know why Mum and Grandma fell out with each other?'

'Don't know the full story. I know something happened to your mum, something that Gran would never talk about. Dad and Jack sometimes said things like "Wonder if Ellie's happy" or "Wonder if she made the right decision." I can tell you this for nothing, back then fellas could do whatever they liked to a girl and she'd get the blame. The gossip would be all about her, never the man. We're a bit more enlightened now. It's my understanding that things got out of hand between your mother and Grandma because they couldn't see eye to eye about your dad, but there's prob'ly more to it than that.'

'Both Mum and Grandpa have mentioned Kate. Sounds like she was kind to Mum.'

'That's Grandpa's sister. She lived at Oban, but she died some years ago.'

# 38

We walked the road to the old church that, according to Claire, now waited in swampy ground for Friday night bingo fans and Saturday dancers.

Claire told me that when she was young, sometimes bold boys and adventurous girls lowered themselves over the bridge wall onto a fat water pipe that ran the length of the arch before burying itself in the peaty banks on each side. 'They'd grasp the parapet and inch their way along to the other side but usually get caught by Father Hammil or his housekeeper, who lived in that old house.' She pointed to a cottage about thirty metres away.

Claire said she'd made arrangements elsewhere for the rest of the day and, as I had planned to see Fiona, we parted company at the corner of Vale Street. I carried on alone. I walked along the riverside and the only sounds were wind through tips of trees, rushing water, and an occasional bird call. No hint of human voice. I walked for almost an hour and when I got back to Grandma's they were reading in the living room.

'The woman in the library is a friendly soul,' I said. 'And the gardens around here are so well kept and colourful.'

Grandpa raised his eyebrows in a question mark. 'Well now, Anna, I saw an ad for a wee house for sale two streets away. Maybe you'd like tae settle doon here. It seems tae me that you're at a crossroads in your life and maybe a few years in Scotland would set you on the right track for the coming years. Besides, it would be real nice to have you near us.'

'That's a big question, Grandpa. And you're right: I don't have any plans other than the next few months. But you never know how things'll turn out. For now I'm off across the oval to see Fiona.'

**39**

When Fiona opened her door to me, an appetising smell of curry wafted across my nose. The house was quiet – only the faint sound of instrumental music from somewhere along the hallway.

'C'mon in, Anna. I've been looking forward to havin' the chance tae spend some time wi' you.' She had a wooden spoon in her right hand and a warm welcoming smile lit up her eyes. Her face was pale, round, and her complexion looked like satin. Her glasses, smudged with what looked like flour, had slipped to the end of her nose and her hair was tied back with a red chiffon scarf that fell over her shoulders. A white long-sleeved shirt and casual black pants were almost protected by an apron hanging loosely around her neck. It was stained with something that could have been tomato sauce or strawberries. Among these smudges, a slogan.

I laughed when I read, 'To Hell with Housework, I'm off to the Dancing.'

'Hi, Fiona. How are you? Love the apron.'

She showed me into the kitchen, asked what I'd like to drink, and poured us both a glass of red wine. While she fussed over steamers and casserole dishes, I sat at the table. Between sips of wine and chopping vegies, she talked about her work as national union representative for the nursing industry.

As she cleaned off a bench top she said, 'I'm having a few days off. I'm hoping that maybe you and me could spend some time together.'

'I'd like that, and I like that music. What is it?'

She left the room for a minute, came back with a CD case and handed it to me. 'It's the Gaelforce Orchestra playing a' the old Scottish songs, softly, the way I like to hear them.'

Fiona's voice was warm and soft, with a smile in every sentence. She asked me if I knew that Mum had phoned her a few weeks before she died.

'Yeah, I know about that and I know also that you and she ran away when you were young.'

Her laugh sounded to me like it was coming from the heart of her. 'Och – such a time we had –a lot o' water's gone under the bridge since those days, I tell you.'

'Tell me about it. Why did you? What did your parents say?'

It looked to me like she was preparing enough food for an army of hungry folk and while she busied herself with things on the stove and in the sink, she told me about an escapade to London when she and Mum were sixteen.

'Well, it was like this,' she said. 'Your mam was sick of her job in the local draper's shop, and sick of listening to her mother's criticisms about her manners and hairstyle, so she talked me into runnin' away to London with 'er. It was a soft night in early summer and it was nearly dark when we left. We met near the sleepers by the railway siding. I told your mam that old Ashwood, an old village worthie, had been watchin' ahint his curtains. Mr Ashwood, he's dead now, was known as News o' the World, loved gossip. He used to hang over his garden gate an' watch the villagers move about their business. He knew who lived where, who was married to whom, who could be trusted, who couldn't be, an' whose reputation survived in the talk o' men in the pub. Elner told me off for usin' words like "ahint". She said that if we were hopin' tae get jobs in London we'd need to speak proper English. I told her she was a snob and that you'd never know we'd gone tae the same school.'

Fiona then told me that the main reason they'd chosen London was that they fancied themselves in knee-high boots and mini skirts like they'd seen Twiggy wearing in magazines. They'd been practising singing 'Walking Back to Happiness' like Helen Shapiro and the plan was to get any kind of work, take singing lessons, get themselves discovered and become famous with their faces on the covers of record albums.

'Back then, all your mam wanted was to live free from this place. She began to feel that she was bein' held too tight to the conventions and creeds o' Catholicism. She wanted to meet people who knew about the world outside our village. We'd talked about travellin' to places like the Canadian Rockies or the Australian bush and we'd read about people hiking in the Himalayas. That night Elner had brought a bunch o' flowers from the garden on her way out an' while we waited for the bus we made circlets from the flowers and put one on each o' our heads. We sang a parody of a hymn we used to sing in the May processions. I still remember the words.'

Mum had told me about these church events when they'd parade from the school to the church. Girls dressed in white satin with bridal veils flowing over their shoulders from coronets of wax orange blossom. Boys wore dark trousers, white shirts and red sashes.

Fiona stopped chopping to pour us more wine. She stood straight and tall with her left hand sitting gently on the palm of her right hand. With her shoulders back and looking straight ahead, she started to sing. 'Bring flowers of the fairest…bring blossoms the rarest… Our poor hearts are swelling, our glad voices telling…the praise of the loveliest flowers of the vale.'

I was sitting in a kitchen a million miles from my life, among cooking smells and sizzling saucepans, listening awestruck to a middle-aged woman sing with the innocence of a child. Her voice hit the ceiling and came back again. I wanted to cry.

The last word faded. Fiona stood silent, staring into space. Her face reminded me of the look I'd seen on Mum's face during those first weeks of the last bit of her life. It was a time when she seemed to fall back into more and more of the past.

When she'd talked about her childhood, her voice had gathered strength, and her face took on the look of the young girl she'd once been. That same transformation I now saw in Fiona.

'You know, Anna, when I think about it, I believe we sang our childhood away into that night.'

'Why do you say that? What happened?'

Fiona turned away from her thoughts. 'Och well, we just seemed to grow up too quick that year. Nothin' sinister happened that time, or the time we nearly went tae America, but...'

I spluttered on my drink. 'What do you mean, America?

'I'll tell you about that when I've finished talkin' about the London adventure.' She sat down opposite me.

'We arrived at Central Station after ten that night. A cleaner in dirty overalls sweepin' the concourse was the only sign of activity. He gave our crowns a strange look, like he'd never seen anybody wi' flowers in their hair before. When we asked what time the next train left for London. He mumbled, T"Ten o'clock the morra mornin'," an' the cigarette at the corner of his mouth jiggled up an' down. The tearooms an' newsagent shops were closed an' the doorway tae the public toilets was padlocked. By that time, our haversacks were beginnin' to feel very, very heavy an' I didn't feel too good either. We used up some time lookin' in shop windows in the nearby streets and killed more havin' a rest on a bench in George Square, before wanderin' back tae the station.

'I remember seeing posters stuck tae a shop window advertisin' hazelnut toffee an' Cadburys chocolate and my mouth watered at the sight. I found the biscuits I'd packed in a wee compartment o' my bag. They'd been pressin' against my back giving me a pain. They were broken into bits so we ate most of the broken bits and scattered the crumbs for starlings roosting in the rafters. Your mother said if we were kind to the birds, things would turn out okay for us. I told her that she was too much of a dreamer that things don't always turn out the way we want them to.

'We were really tired by then so we made pillows of our bags, buttoned the toggles on our duffle coats an' spent the night tryin' to bend our bodies into the shape of the station benches. After an agony of tossin' and bruisin' against the iron sides, your mam gave up. She sat cross-legged on her bag on the floor, restin' her head on folded arms at the edge of the seat. When we woke up, a man in LMS uniform was standin' over us. He asked where we were headed. When I told him London, he got real narky and said we should've booked a room at the YWCA just round the corner. I was annoyed at the thought that we'd missed out on a comfortable bed.'

# 40

The bell on the oven rang at that point and Fiona jumped up to attend to it. She put oven mitts on and, talking above the noise of glass on metal, brought two dishes out of the oven, shuffled two more in and went on with her story.

'We'd booked accommodation in a youth hostel near Euston Station in London. We arrived about seven o'clock that evening. The woman in charge was really snotty. "You are only allowed to stay here for two weeks," she told us in a voice that sounded like the Queen Mother, and sniffed up her nose when she saw our wrinkled clothes and tired faces. "D'you have a kitchen here where we can make oursel's a meal?" I asked. "Absolutely not!" she shouted. So the first thing we did was go to a wee restaurant around the corner and paid a fortune for fish that looked like the sole of my shoe and chips like sticks of cinnamon. Then we went to Trafalgar Square and let the pigeons sit on our arms and heads.

'By the end of the second day we'd spent what we'd considered would keep us for a week. We'd wanted to go to Windsor Castle but we couldn't work out the tube system, or how to get anywhere by bus or understand the Cockney accents of the taxi drivers. We didn't like the crowds, the noises or the smells. The pain in my back got worse an' I couldn't eat. We only stayed in London two days an' two nights. Your mam hated to give up. We knew we'd have tae face the wrath of our parents, but London was all too hard for us. That was our first venture into the big world beyond this village. It turned out that I had pleurisy and was confined to bed for six weeks. Your mam was allowed to visit me an' I told her she could travel wherever she wanted but this place would do me fine.'

Fiona stopped stirring something in a saucepan, looked over at me and said, 'Your mam was a great one for writing things down. I want to talk to you about that, but we'll have a bit of dinner first.'

While she spooned sauces into bowls and sorted utensils, I asked her to tell me about nearly going to America.

'Och, that surely was a hare-brained scheme if ever we had one. Your mam spotted an ad in the Glasgow *Herald* seekin' nannies for a psychologist's family in Philadelphia. So we made an appointment with the American consulate in Glasgow. The officer looked at our birth certificates, smiled and sent us home wi' advice to try again when we were eighteen an' had a letter of consent from our parents. The interview lasted less than ten minutes. After that disappointment we talked about joinin' the navy but again you had to be eighteen an' so we'd decided London was far enough an' you know how that ended up. Now tell me, did your mam have a happy life wi' Peter?'

I told Fiona about the music Mum and Dad played – usually Celtic folk songs by the Galliards, or ballads like Harry Belafonte's 'Scarlet Ribbons', or Ella Fitzgerald's 'With a Song in My Heart'. And how, before Dad died, they'd sing in harmony and dance around the house.

'Y'know, Fiona, Dad used to stick a rose behind Mum's ear and they'd dance for three or four songs doing exaggerated tango movements from one end of the lounge to the other. And when they'd put on Scottish dance music and do a jig like a couple of teenagers, I'd think they were being silly and go to the kitchen or my bedroom.'

Fiona laughed. 'I'm so happy that her life wi' Peter turned out okay. It gives my heart a treat to hear that.'

## 41

The dining room table gleamed with silverware and red-stemmed goblets on top of linen that looked like it had been dipped in silver. One wall supported a gallery of photos of Fiona's children and grandchildren. Their smiling faces in odd-shaped frames covered about a third of the wall space. A print of Gainsborough's *Cottage Girl* in an ornate frame dominated another wall above a cream-coloured leather couch, and a display cabinet in a corner protected trophies and mementoes of her children's sporting achievements.

We settled down to a feast of butter chicken, fish tikkas, curried vegetables, poppadoms, sauces and lovely wine. I felt somehow that I'd been in this comfortable, hospitable place before. While we ate, I learned that she and Mum had started school on the same day and that by the time they'd reached their teens, they were inseparable. They wore similar clothes, sang the same songs, and on weekends they rode their bikes around the hills and lanes together. They spent hours in each other's houses getting ready for dancing on Saturday nights.

'What happened between Mum and Grandma?' I asked. 'Do you know why Mum hated her mother?'

'Oh now, I think hated is too strong a word for what went on between them, Anna. It was more like two single-minded people caught up in a battle of wills. They had the same strength o' conviction but had placed it in a different understandin' o' how they wanted the world to be.'

While Fiona talked, she offered food to me and refilled my wine glass. I was beginning to feel like I'd burst.

'So what happened? How could...'

'They always had their differences about speakin' properly an' things like table manners and bein' ladylike, but these were just minor spats, normal growin' up stuff. The thing that made them enemies all started at the time your mother and father met. It was never the same after that.'

'Why? What was wrong with Dad?

'Well, ye see, Anna, he was not o' the faith, an' that didn't fit wi' your grandmother's beliefs.'

'Mum wrote something about this before she died, but I didn't think it would've been enough reason to cause a permanent rift between them.'

'No,' Fiona said, 'other things happened, but I'll get us some dessert and I'll tell you about the day your parents met.'

Fiona was still talking as she went to the kitchen. The first words I heard when she returned with an apple pie about fifteen centimetres high above the rim of the dish were 'D'you know what happened to your mam in 1964?

'No, I don't. That's one of the reasons I've come here. I didn't even know I had family here until a few months ago.'

'I can't believe she never talked about that night.' She poured tea for both of us while she talked. 'Okay, but when I've finished, we'll talk then about more serious matters.'

We settled down and Fiona told me her version of a day in 1963:

'Your mam and I had gone by bus to Dunoon. We thought we were God's gift to the world, in our stiletto heels and seer-sucker shirt-waisters. A protest march about the Polaris nuclear submarine base in the Holy Loch was on, an' the place was packed wi' demonstrators carryin' placards declarin' things like "Why Choose Us?" and "Yankee Go Home".' Fiona stood tall, raised one arm in the air and shouted the declarations to the ceiling before carrying on. 'We weren't interested in capitalist power or communist Russia – we'd gone for a good time, to wave banners and sing. We'd talked about maybe meetin' rich American sailors who'd fall madly in love wi' us an' carry us off to a life o' luxury in Kentucky or Texas. Your mam kept lookin' at the scenery

and sayin' things about purple mists and shadows on the mountains –
she was such a dreamer. Anyway, on that day, hundreds o' onlookers
lined the shoreline.'

'I've read about this, Fiona. I found newspaper articles in an old
suitcase.'

'Is that right? Wonder why she…och, never mind. Anyway, we
moved to where people were watchin' from the shore an' jostled our way
to the front o' the crowd. A woman in front of us telling her neighbour,
"The young folk o' this toon will get fat sittin' aroon ice-cream parlours
eatin' hot dogs." She wagged her finger and carried on like a fishwife at
the gutting bench. Elner and me just smirked at her. I said to your mam,
"Mary Lou, when yawl goin' home to Narth Carlina?" and the woman
drew daggers at us from two slits of eyes. We moved away before she
thumped us.'

'Your American accent, Fiona…' I burst out laughing.

'Och, it was only a bit o' fun. Anyway, after a few minutes listenin'
to people shoutin' towards the action on the water, I told Elner I was
feelin' sick – I've never liked crowds much. We decided to do a bit o'
window shoppin' along Argyll Street. I spied a canvas tent wi' a sign
sayin' "Let Madam Zara Tell Your Fortune for only 2/6". We decided
to spend the last o' our money (except for chip money an' our fare
home), to hear about our future. Your mam let me go first. I still
remember the smell o' that tent, it was stuffy an' Madam Zara smelled
o' garlic. She had on a purple an' green caftan that started from just
under her chin, then fell in wrinkled folds tae her feet. I think it was
made for two. It took the old witch two tries to spread a fan o' cards
across the table. Some got stuck on bits o' old food dotted on the cloth
like so many dead flies. She told me I'd be married within two years.
She told your mam she'd be married more than once an' she'd travel to
other countries. Your mam said it was a load o' bunkum.' Fiona threw
back her head and chortled.

I laughed with her and pushed my half-eaten apple pie as far away
from my mouth as I could get it. 'I can't believe Mum would ever

spend money on a fortune teller. She was so practical. Fiona, are you dreaming this up for my entertainment?'

'Och, away you go, Anna, this is the god's honest truth.' She sipped and talked and giggled through the rest of the story. 'We were a pair o' silly teenagers sittin' on a bench by the water's edge eatin' chips soaked in vinegar an' retellin' our fortunes to each other when a man wi' a smiling face an' torn jacket came towards us. He'd separated himself from a group o' tired protesters, sprawlin' on nearby lawns amongst the remains o' banners an' handbills. I said to your mam, 'Here's your first man, Elner.,' We laughed like hyenas. But I noticed your mam never took her eyes off him for a second. They seemed tae fit like a hand in a glove from the very first instant.'

'What happened next?' I asked.

'Well, the next thing was, we introduced oursel's tae each other — he said his name was Peter an' asked us to share the joke. I said, "Can't do that but we can share our chips." He asked what were we doin' in Dunoon an' your mam told him we were only down for the day to share in the fun. Peter and your mam gazed at each other the whole time. Your Dad had driven the group o' rebels up from Newcastle in a kombi van an' they'd hardly slept for two nights and days. He asked us if we were goin' home by the same ferry as his group an' we agreed to find each other on board but I knew it was only your mam he wanted to find. I was beginnin' to feel like a gooseberry.'

'What's a...?'

'It's like feelin' a bit out o' place. Your mam and dad were so taken wi' each other an' I felt like I was on the outside lookin' in. The weather was perfect that day, an' the ferry was packed wi' people carryin' baskets and coats. Children ran aroun' tryin' tae take flight wi' the help o' those wee plastic windmills you see at fairgrounds. I didn't like lookin' at the water so I wandered down the gangway tae get us a cup o' tea an' left your mam takin' in the view. When I came back, Peter was standin' beside her. They were talkin' about how some o' the canoes had capsized. Arrests had been made. 'Before the ferry docked at Gourock, they'd arranged tae write tae each other. That was the start o' their tuppence haipenny romance.

'Tuppence…?'

'Och, that was the cost o' postage on a letter in they days… Be back in a sec.'

I heard her feet thump down the hallway.

**42**

When Fiona came back to the lounge, she looked anxious. She fiddled with her hair and the collar of her blouse. It was like she was bothered with some kind of itch or maybe a fly was buzzing around her head and face. She sat down beside me.

The music I'd heard earlier had stopped and all I could hear was the sound of Fiona's agitated breathing.

She started talking. 'It was like this, Anna. Your gran got worried when Ellie got letters and a Valentine card from Peter – although she didn't know who Peter was at the time. Anyway, she started a campaign to get your mam to go out wi' some o' the local boys. 'She said to Ellie, "That boy Ferguson is a nice boy and he wants to go out wi' you."'

Fiona stuck out her chest, her eyes took on a forbidding look and her voice deepened in a parody of an imperious older woman. I smiled at her efforts.

'Ellie told her that if he didn't have the gumption to say that to her face, she wouldn't go out wi' him. Anyway, she couldn't stand him.'

I looked at Fiona. 'Who's John Ferguson?'

'Well, he'd gone to school same time as us. He was a nice boy… on the quiet side. But he wasn't very good-lookin' an' he was a rotten dancer. He was tall an' lanky, like a long drink o' water, an' his hair was the colour o' carrots. His ears stuck out like wings, an' we used tae say if he flapped them real hard, he'd take flight. I know that was cruel. I just hope he never heard us. Mind you, he was smart – always top o' the class in school an' ended up runnin' his own civil engineerin' company. I heard recently that he's been workin' on the new houses o' parliament in Edinburgh, in cahoots wi' the Catalan architect Enric Miralles.'

'I'm glad to hear that Mum's rejection didn't hold him back.'

Fiona laughed. 'Well, eventually your mam agreed to go out wi' Frank Welsh. He was very good-looking and a great dancer but a bit o' a sleazebag – at least that's what I thought o' him. Another lassie in the village had gone out wi' him and she'd told me that he was a bit pushy when it came to saying goodnight. I told Ellie this but she wanted to get on the good side o' her mother. Because he was the head altar boy at St Conval's, this would do the trick in mother/daughter relationships. Jimmy Bogle, my ex, invited me tae the St Patrick's night dance so the four of us teamed up.

'The night o' that dance, things started out okay. Jimmy an' Frank Welsh met us at your gran's place. She was so pleased that Ellie had finally agreed to go out wi' a nice Catholic boy as everybody thought he was. I remember she beamed at the four of us. "Have a good time," she said. Frank told your mam she looked great but he was lookin' her up an' down like a lecher as he said that, an' I remember thinkin' what a creep he was. When we got to the dance, Frank went straight to the bar an' when your mam chose to drink orangeade instead of whisky, he got real huffy an' hardly spoke to us after that. The music was a mix of folksy Celtic stuff an' rock 'n roll. In those days it was the done thing for a bunch o' lassies tae dance together so we didn't really need partners an' we were havin' a good time.

'The night was more than halfway through when I noticed your mam an' Frank Welsh had disappeared. I looked in the ladies room an' the cloakroom for her, but her coat had gone. She'd left without sayin' cheerio an' that was no' like her. I left Jimmy dancin' wi' somebody else and walked home. I'll never forget what met me when I turned in at our gate.'

At this point Fiona stood up. She started pacing up and down. Rolling her sleeves up. Rolling them down. All the while pacing. Pacing and talking. She carried on in a voice that sounded as if the words were fighting their way through a bucket of rusty nails.

'I heard a voice say "Fiona, Fiona" in a loud whisper. Your mam was hidin' behind the front hedge. She was sobbin' her heart out an' tryin 'to comb her hair with her hands. Her dress an' coat were mucky and wrinkled. She was in a terrible state. I got her inside an' into my bedroom. When I asked her who'd did this tae her, she said, "Who do you think?" I said then that I was goin' over tae get her mother an' she begged me not to. She held on to my arms an' cried. She thought her mother would blame her. I said to her then, "He's no' gettin' away wi' this. I'm goin' to tell Father O'Malley," an' she said nobody was to know, that I was the only person she could trust. In the end I agreed to keep it between us an' fetched a facecloth an' basin o' water to help cool her swollen eyes. I gave her a dressin' gown to put on while I cleaned up her clothes as best as I could an' we sat whisperin' an' cryin' for such a long while. We concocted a story that would answer any questions her ma 'n' da might ask about her bein' out so late.'

By the time Fiona reached this part of the story, tears were sliding down her face and a pile of tissues lay on the floor between our feet.

'When I watched Elner limp across the oval that night, my heart broke in two for her. But the horror didn't stop that night.'

'What d'you mean? What don't I know? What happened to Mum?'

'Well, disaster struck sometime in April. She came across to me at breakfast time and signalled that she wanted to talk to me in my room. Ye see, Anna, the worst wrong thing a girl could do in this village back then was to get pregnant before marriage an' it was always the fault of the girl. The next worst thing was a Catholic girl havin' an English Protestant for a boy friend. Any mix o' religion was considered heresy.

'Your mam had felt queasy when she got out o' bed that mornin' an' had to run to the bathroom, an' when I opened the door to her, the colour had drained from her face an' left it white as milk. She sat down on my bed an' put her head between her knees an' she told me that she might be pregnant. We both cried a bucketful. She was plannin' on tellin' her mother the next day an' I said I'd stand beside her tae give her a bit o' courage. What a terrible thing it was tae witness your gran's hysteria and rage. She lost her composure that day, I can tell you.

'Your mam an' I stood in the livin' room like two lumps o' stone.

Your gran was cleanin' the windows an' had a bucket o' water on a wee stepladder. She heard the word "pregnant", and screeched, "Holy mother of Jesus!" gasping the words while her face changed shape, like she'd tasted bitter aloes. Her lips narrowed into straight lines an' stayed that way for the longest time. Then she lifted the wet cloth an' swung it across your mam's face. Some o' the water splattered on to me an' my legs went soft like jelly.'

'What did Mum do?'

'Well, I left her standin' starin' at your gran, an' waited at the front door. Eventually, she came an' told me to go home, that she'd talk to me later. That same day Elner told her parents that she'd never marry Frank Welsh an' as far as your gran was concerned, that meant war. The only way she knew how to fight, besides naggin' the life out o' your mother, was to sprinkle holy water around the house and light candles in front o' a wee statue of St Jude, the patron saint o' hopeless cases.

'She went to Mass every mornin' and made a novena to him. When Saint Jude failed tae get your mam tae see her mother's way of things, your gran appealed tae Father O'Malley. That's how it was then, Anna, the priest was a power in a small community like this. He told your mam that it was a terrible thing to bring an illegitimate child into this world, and he asked her to think o' the pain she was causin' her mother an' the Blessed Virgin Mary. Can you believe that?'

I didn't know what to believe. I was finding it hard to comprehend everything I was hearing. Stilted unfinished thoughts and questions skittered across my mind like speeding traffic on a freeway.

Then I remembered the words Mum had written to me on her death bed. 'Anna, so much in my life you know nothing about. Judge me kindly.'

Fiona disappeared. She returned a minute later with two glasses of soda water. 'Here, drink this, Anna. It'll help tae clear your mind a bit.'

'Do I have a brother or sister somewhere?'

'No, Anna, your mam did get pregnant but it's a long, sad story and, tae tell ye the honest truth, she never did tell me the details. All I knew back then is that it was the worst time in Ellie's life.' Fiona's voice was hoarse by now.

'You look tired, Fiona. I should go and let you get to bed.' I gathered up my bag and put my jacket on.

We said goodnight with a promise to talk more. It was two o'clock in the morning when I crossed the oval. My grandparents were asleep. My head was full to the brim with what Fiona had told me. I needed to be alone to think about it all. I fell asleep with my head on a wet pillow.

**43**

The sun was high in the sky when I woke up next morning. The house was silent. A note on the kitchen table told me that my grandparents would be at Jack's place at West Kilbride for the day.

I sat in the garden for a while listening to the sounds of the village. I heard someone thumping scales on an out-of-tune piano in the house next door, and watched two young boys chasing birds from the oval with ammunition fired from slingshots.

After showering and breakfast, I decided to hire a car and take a drive to Dunoon.

While waiting for the car to be delivered, I packed some bread, cheese, fruit and water. The hire car rep gave me maps of the area and showed me the best route.

I set off on the main road south from the village then turned west towards Gourock. It was easy driving on the highway, until I reached the hilly town of Port Glasgow, where I took a wrong turn at one of the many twists and bends. After driving around winding streets for ten minutes, I pulled to the side of the road, and beckoned to an elderly couple walking towards me.

I said to the woman, 'Hi. Could you point me in the direction of the dockside?'

The man mumbled something that began 'Och now, she disnae ken…'

I lost him after that but the gist was the woman had no idea. With a lot of finger pointing and arm sweeping, from the man, I finally understood that I was only round the corner from my goal. It took less than five minutes to park the car, buy my ticket and board.

During the half-hour ferry trip, I wandered along the gangway eavesdropping on tourist conversations about B&B places, good sightseeing destinations and the price of petrol. I saw a young couple with their arms around each other and thought about Mum and Dad standing at that same spot in 1963, perhaps facing the same scene. Then I remembered how Mum had looked as she was dying and turned my head away. I nearly changed my mind and got off the ferry, but just then it started moving.

The hills around Dunoon dipped down to rolling farmlands and the deep clean water of the Kyles of Bute. Beyond the hills I could see shadows of mountains humped high on the horizon. Houses dotted beyond the shoreline were white and shining in the sun. In shelters along the promenade, people were eating and children ran around with puffy sticks of candy floss.

When I disembarked, I walked along busy streets between shops to a little hill on the outskirts of the town and sat beneath the spreading branches of a chestnut tree. The sun had warmed the air and brought the hills closer. The surface of the water lay like a mirror pocked by little puffs of wind.

After eating my lunch, I walked through the town looking at the faces passing by and tried to capture the ethos of romance in the middle of a protest march in the 1960s. I didn't see any protesters, or canoes skimming the water, or fortune-tellers. I did get a whiff of fish and chips. It seemed to me that someone or something had washed the colour from the town that Fiona had described to me.

An hour later I was on the return ferry. I didn't bother to look at the view.

## 44

On the return trip to Glenhill, other drivers honked and shouted abuse at my inept navigating skills. I was glad to get back to the familiar streets and park the car. A good stretch of the legs was what I needed. I set off to follow the shape of the river and soon filled my lungs with air scented by fir and pine.

A short distance to the north of the chapel, a range of hills cradled the village in its bulbous care as if protecting it from unseen danger. At the edge of a patch of rhododendrons, the pathway climbed to an intersection with an asphalt road. The far side was held against the side of a hill by a dry-stone wall. I noticed something on the face of the hill glinting in the sunlight.

As I drew nearer, it took the shape of a drinking cup chained to a well. A giant chrome-plated water tap was bricked into the wall. An inscription read, 'Rest and be Thankful.' A constant trickle of water drained into the basin below it and presumably ended up in the river I'd just walked beside. Tasting the clean cold water turned my parched throat into a conduit of euphoria that spread from my finger tips to my toes.

Beside the well, a wrought-iron seat commemorating the life of one Douglas McCarron was a handy resting place where I could look over the whole valley. I imagined the gales that would batter this place in winter and pictured the tree branches hanging on to the trunks the way frightened children hold tightly to a protective parent.

I thought if I could view the glen below me from the top of a mountain it would look like the palm of a giant hand. Four narrow roads and the river formed fingers of travel that led to other towns and villages. The river had its source high up in the mountains behind where I sat. I imagined crystal water flowing around pine forests, scouring deep ravines and leaving little pools of foam and silent ponds where river creatures could live and breed. Compared to the brown sluggish Torrens that flowed near my part of Adelaide, this was Eden. I tried to spot Gran's house at the northern end of the road that led to Glasgow. I couldn't get the orientation right.

My reverie was disturbed by the noise of tramping feet from a group of chattering hikers with backpacks, long poles and sturdy boots that popped out from the edge of the woods as if they'd fallen from the trees. They chorused, 'Good morning.'

While filling water bottles from the well, their leader asked me, 'Are you on a pilgrimage too?'

'Kind of.'

'Well, good luck wi' your journey and safe home to wherever that is.'

I left them chatting amongst themselves about the next stage of their adventure and set off back to the village. It took me almost an hour to find my way back.

**45**

I popped in to see Fiona and tell her about my jaunt. 'Would you like to come for a drive to Oban tomorrow?' I asked.

'I'd love that, Anna. Have you got time for a cup o' tea, an' a wee slice o' apple pie?

'Sure,' I said, taking off my jacket and settling down at the kitchen table.

Fiona's idea of a 'wee slice' almost filled the plate she put it on. Then she topped it with a dollop of thick cream that slithered to the rim of the plate. She sat across the table from me, moved a bowl of fruit to one side and poured tea for both of us.

I asked her to tell me about the last time she'd seen Mum.

'I know exactly when. It was the seventeenth of June 1964. I remember the date because it was my father's birthday.'

Fiona twisted her chair to the side, settled her feet and legs across another chair, folded her arms and half shut her eyes. I settled opposite her – I was in for another long yarn.

'I didn't know your mam an' dad were comin' that day an' I was busy in the kitchen helpin' my mother bakin' some cakes for visitors we were expectin' that afternoon. The doorbell rang an' the next thing I heard was Ellie's voice in the hallway asking if I was home. Well, you could've blown me away wi' a feather. She looked wonderful. The pale face an' black shadows aroun' her eyes that she'd left wi' had disappeared. Her face glowed wi' health an' her eyes sparkled. She looked like she'd spent the past while in some kind o' paradise. She wore a white dress made wi' cambric. It was straight, sleeveless an' had one o' those wee mandarin collars. Her hair shone like a new penny an' hung loose down her back. She carried what we called then, a picture hat wi' the widest brim. It was white too, an' trimmed wi' pale green satin ribbon.

'We stood like doolies lookin' at each other, an' then we started laughing. It was so good to see her lookin' happy. She told me Peter wanted to meet her mother. He wanted to reassure your gran that he would care for Elner, an' he wanted them to be friends. He'd stayed in the car an' when I went out to say hello to him, we agreed that it'd be best if he went for a wee drive around the village while your mam went in to break the ice. I said I'd go across wi' her thinkin' it would make things easier for your mother and grandmother.

'Talk about calamity! I've never forgotten how they looked at each other that day. Your gran was standin' at the kitchen bench rollin' pastry. Her hands were covered in flour an' I could smell some meat dish cooking on the stove. Elner an' your grandad stood in the doorway. I stood beside them. Your gran carried on rolling for a wee while, an' then she turned to face us. I nearly shrivelled into nothin' the way she glared at me but I didn't move so she turned her stare on your mam. They looked at each other like they were in some kind of contest. Elner said, in a quiet determined way, that Peter would like to meet her.

'That's when hell broke loose an' your gran started yellin'. "He will never darken this door! I will never have an English Protestant in my house!" Then she ranted on about saints an' sin…what people would say about Elner…about how good a mother she'd been to her an' she didn't deserve this kind of penance.' While Fiona talked, her arms waved, her eyes widened, her fingers pointed and poked at ghosts, and her voice took on the tone of a tyrant.

I blinked. Tried to imagine my grandmother yelling and wielding a rolling pin the way Fiona described. I reminded myself that she was miming something she'd seen forty years ago. I pulled my eyes away from her and concentrated on the pie and cream.

Then I asked quietly, 'What happened next?'

'Well, blow me down, your gran told Elner to take her man and go. Your grandpa got really agitated, he started fillin' the kettle to make tea, sayin' they should sit down. They didn't seem to hear him.

'Ellie said, "You can keep your Pope and robes and host and chalice –

all I need to make an honest life is Peter." Then she stomped out the door wi' your grandpa behind her. I sneaked a look back at your grandma. She was leanin' against the bench. Then she gathered up the pastry she'd been workin' wi' and tossed it in the bin. She slumped down on a chair wi' her head in her hands. If she was cryin', she was very quiet about it. I wanted to say somethin' but I was scared that she'd start yellin' at me.

'While we waited for Peter to come back, your mam an' I walked back tae here. She said she'd been hopin' that her mother would've learned somethin' from their separation an' everything that had happened. But after the row they'd just had, I think she realised that they'd never see the same way o' lookin' at things that mattered. We said goodbye an' promised to keep in touch, then she walked away from me across the oval to join your grandpa, who stood by his gate waitin' for her an' Peter. When he finally arrived, I saw him shake hands with your grandpa. I stood out there at the gate an' watched your grandpa put his arms around your mam. He gave your dad a package of some kind.'

'I bet that was the packet with the photos and clippings from the old suitcase.'

'That's what I jaloused when you told me about it,' Fiona said.

'The three o' them talked for a wee while, then Ellie and Peter got into the car an' two sad souls, me and your grandpa that is, stood at each side of the oval. We waved as the wee blue Morris turned the corner an' disappeared out o' sight.'

Fiona sighed, picked up our cups and plates and stuck them in the dishwasher. Her voice sounded faraway, like an echo. 'That's the last time I saw your mam.'

I got up from the table, walked through to the living room and looked across the oval. I tried hard to see what Fiona had seen that day but saw only a small group of men standing in a corner and a little boy being taught how to ride a bike.

'I'm so sorry she never kept in touch with you, Fiona,' I said when I went back to join her. 'I've no explanation for that. She did talk about you,' I lied. 'She thought the world of you.'

'Och, I know. That kind of friendship doesn't die wi' time and distance, but in a lot o' ways it was best that your mam cut all ties. She had a lot o' livin' to do an' she couldn't do it here. This place was too hard on her soul.'

I thought about that last phrase – too hard on her soul – and came to the conclusion that the rape of my mother, the pregnancy, all of that, had served as a disastrous catalyst that created a pathway for her escape from a place she'd outgrown.

I asked Fiona if she'd be ready to leave for Oban by ten-thirty in the morning and crossed the oval to check on my grandparents. They hadn't returned from Jack's place and I set off walking along the road to the church where Claire and I had walked.

<h1 align="center">46</h1>

The road north from the village followed the course of the river, slicing through fields of wheat, potatoes and turnip. Just past the last house, a small bridge rose on the east side of the river and fell down on the west – a span of about ten metres. Waist-high stone walls spanned each side of the bridge. Even the smallest child could find a foothold to climb high enough and peer over at the water. I could see near the river's edge, where mossy stones broke the surface. The shallow water just covered rounded pebbles with its fast flowing currents. The soggy boggy shore was home to frogs and eels and an occasional trout hid in fronds of willow trees and water lilies.

A paddock close by was thick with bramble bushes and wild fat hairy gooseberries. Grandpa had told me in his younger days he'd come to this spot to 'guddle trout for that night's dinner'. When I asked him what he meant by 'guddle', he'd laughed and said he'd show me 'yin o' these days'.

The bridge allowed parishioners access to the old church of St Conval, now a social club where bingo and birthdays were celebrated. A new church had been built at the other end of the village. Claire had told me that what used to be the confessional boxes in the old church were now toilets marked 'LASSIES' and 'LADDIES'. We'd sniggered at the irony of so much guilt and forgiveness steeped in the walls.

When I'd seen this part of the village with Claire, the sound of the river running over rocks and under the bridge had signified freedom. Now I saw the greenness as a swamp where evil had stalked. Looking across the paddock from the bridge to the priest's house, I thought about my mother. I thought about the violation she'd suffered somewhere in that murky patch. Why hadn't she punched and kicked and spat, gouged his eyes, stuck a stiletto heel in his foot, thrust a knee into his groin and watched him vomit?

I stood on the bridge for a while then wandered back to the library to check my mail.

Joe: 'Still missing you. Do they have email in the frozen north?'

Mardi: 'Are you still alive? It would be nice to hear from you!'

After a quick response to both of them, I got home just in time to help Grandma out of Jack's car. Over a light supper of tasty oat cakes, cheese and jam, we spent the evening telling each other about the day's exploits. I told them a bit about my interests in history and before he went to bed, Grandpa gave me his copy of *The Jacobite Rebellion* by D.K. Broster. 1745 – The last war fought on British soil. The text was scattered with words I'd no hope of pronouncing (how do you say Bein Laoigh?). A glossary on ancient Scottish words would've been useful. I read about a close-knit Highland community embroiled in civil war. The work included the lovers Alison and Lachlan, who used phrases like 'dear heart' and 'beloved of mine' to express their feelings. I smiled when I remembered Joe's rough hewn and rare words of well-meant affection.

The connections with England in the time of Cromwell and Charles I was something I knew about. But the furore and dissension that the King's imposition of a new prayer book had caused the people of Scotland was less familiar to me.

The book slid to the floor and next thing I knew the sun was blaring its way through a chink in the curtains. The first thought in my mind was Joe: what is he doing right now? Does he think about me? Where are you, my king-hearted friend?

The book lay where it had fallen. I picked it up, found the last words I'd read and snuggled into the blankets.

An hour later, I heard Grandpa and Fiona talking at the front door and made a mad dash for the bathroom.

## 47

The extended McCrae family used Kate's house at Oban as a holiday place. Grandpa gave me the keys and Fiona and I set off a little later than planned. Soon we crossed the Erskine Bridge and passed the ramparts of Dumbarton castle. Fiona started singing at the top of her voice and by the time we stopped at the Sly Poacher's cafe in the village of Luss for lunch, I was singing along with her about high roads, low roads and bonnie banks.

I have never tasted salmon so sweet, so succulent. Lightly poached and served with dill sauce, the fish seemed to have jumped from the river onto my plate. I said this to Fiona.

'Well, Anna,' she quipped, 'the Erskine River's only a few miles from here and Scotland's full o' surprises.'

Her expression changed when I asked, 'What happened to your marriage, Fiona?'

'Well, to tell you the honest truth, Anna, I don't know. One day I was married to a handsome honest man, and before I knew it he'd turned into an ugly squat toad, wi' wrinkles and a sour temperament and I decided to make my escape before I began to look like him.'

The road we travelled after lunch was like a ribbon thrown carelessly around mountains that dominated the countryside and reached high above the treeline. We passed fields covered in moss and lichen so thick it looked like you'd sink in it up to your knees.

Fiona's light-heartedness made it easy for me to concentrate on the narrow convoluted roads. She'd say, 'Repeat after me,' and pronounce place names on signposts like Crianlarich, Ballochuilish and Drumnadrochit, keeping the 'ch' sound rattling around at the back of her throat as if she was massaging her tonsils.

We laughed ourselves silly at my attempts to get the inflection right.

At one point Fiona started to say, 'Eln…' then, 'Ooops, for a minute I thought I was with your mam.'

We were silent with our own thoughts for the next few kilometres. I saw a sign pointing out the route to Culloden Field and braked suddenly.

Fiona nearly jumped out of her seat. 'What's happenin'? The car stalled, has it?'

'Can't believe it! I read about the Jacobite invasion last night and here we are passing the road to the site where the Highland army was annihilated.'

'Wanna take a detour?

'No, we'll carry on. I'm anxious to get to Oban. Maybe on the way back.' I put the car into gear.

Many of the signs we passed had beguiling names of historical significance, like Tyndrum and the road constructed by General George Wade at the time of the Highland Clearances. In the midst of the Gaelic grandeur and history, we passed a shop signed, 'Ben Wong – Purveyor of Turkish Kebabs and Fish and Chips'. We laughed so loud and long I had to hold tight to the steering wheel.

## 48

The sun was still high in the sky when we reached Oban. I looked around the rooms in Kate's house thinking I'd find hints about how my mother had spent her time. But like footsteps on water, any evidence of her had been destroyed or buried beneath years of holiday accoutrements.

Within minutes, Fiona was in the kitchen opening cupboards and jars and doing a stocktake of tinned fruit and vegetables. 'It looks like these packets of cereals are left over from last summer, Anna. Maybe I can rustle up some pancakes.' She levered the lid from a plastic container of flour. 'Holy Jeesis! This if full o' weevils. We'll have tae do a bit o' shopping.' She put the kettle on, dumped the flour into a plastic bag and, with the boxes of breakfast cereal, took the lot out to the big bin in the yard.

While this was going on, I wandered through the house. Curtain rings had fell away from the fabric, leaving drapes with holes hanging lopsided. A shelf stacked with board games had a pile of Monopoly money scattered on top as if the players had left in angry defeat. I found some clean sheets and blankets in an ottoman at the end of one bed. By the time Fiona had done her darndest to clean out the stock of food, I'd made up two beds and opened all the windows.

Fiona called out to me, 'I've found some decent tea and the kettle's on.'

'Let's have it outside, Fiona. I'll get a tray.'

The rose bushes along the driveway were overgrown and wild. Brown-fringed heads of yellow blooms hung listlessly as if they were too old and tired to look up to the sun. So too were the berry bushes along the back fence. Raspberries had dried and drooped on the sticks as if they were seeking sustenance from the ground beneath them.

A little table and two rickety rattan chairs on the back porch looked like they were crying out for company. I found a small clean tablecloth and we set the pot of tea between us to enjoy the warm, still air.

'Now listen, Anna,' Fiona lectured, 'it's no good a young person like yourself to be living in the past. You want to get out partying a bit more. Get music into your bones!' She stirred three teaspoonfuls of sugar into her tea. 'Tell me, do you have a young fella in your life to distract you frae all the darkness about your mother?'

'Not really. I like Joe and I know he's got feelings for me but at this point we're just friends.'

'Sounds tae me that you'd like it tae be more than that.'

'Yeah maybe, but right now he's at the other end of the earth and he's a bit short on communication skills.'

Fiona laughed. 'Tell you what, Anna, I think we should hit the pubs down on Main Street. They put on a fine Highland ceilidh at the Skipinnish. We'll do a bit o' dancin' and sing some sentimental songs. What d'ye think o' that?'

'Sounds okay to me. But before that, I'd like to prune some of these bushes and maybe tidy up the garden a bit. Besides, it'll be good to spend some time in the open air after being cooped up in the car.'

'Okey dokey. I'll just clear off the tea things and try to make sense of the stuff in the kitchen. The benches need a good wash.'

**49**

Hiding behind bushes at the back of the garden stood an old lopsided shed with gaping wooden slats for walls. I pushed and heaved at the door. It protested against the disturbance, and screeched its way over the gravel at the entrance. Cleaning off enough cobwebs to see the interior challenged my fears of things that crawled and stung. I had to remind myself that probably (probably?), red-back spiders and snakes didn't exist here.

Spades and rakes and garden shears stood like war-weary sentinels against the far wall and a wheelbarrow, handles resting beside the tools, had a deflated perished rubber wheel. Mud-caked gardening gloves in a box proved too solid to be useful. A small tarpaulin made a handy carrier for shears, pruning tools, garden fork and rake. I stacked these onto it, and trailed the load over the weed-filled pathway to the front of the house.

While I teased out the tangled weeds from the roses, my thoughts settled. A feeling of contentment crept over me. The fecund scent of the earth soared up to my senses and I wondered if this was maybe how my mother had spent her days here with Kate.

After a while, Fiona called out, 'You've done a grand job, Anna, that's some pile of weeds, but it's time we cleaned ourselves up and headed down for a night of hilarity.' She stood at the front door, wearing an apron and her sleeves rolled up to the elbows. The pinny had splotches of dirty water that looked like map outlines of unknown territories.

'Won't be long now,' I answered, and started the trek to the backyard. I stacked weeds in a corner and put the tools back where I'd found them.

Shelves and cupboards surrounded the walls of the shed. Faded labels on boxes of assorted sizes were written in scrolled handwriting. It looked like chickens had scratched the words: 'Fertiliser. Mothballs. Paintbrushes.' A box perched above me caught my eye. It had a stencilled warning: 'Handle With Care'. Beneath the caution, 'Eleanor' was written in neat cursive writing and faded black ink.

Just as I reached up to it Fiona shouted again, 'Anna, I've booked a table for seven o'clock. You better get a move on!'

As I turned round and moved towards the door, some force pulled me back as if a linked iron chain held me on the spot.

Fiona called out again. I left the box in its place.

# 50

At Skippinish Ceilidh House we were greeted like long-lost friends by the staff.

'Just the two of you?' a young man in a kilt and Braveheart shirt asked.

'Yes,' Fiona answered.

'Well, perhaps you'd like to join the group over in that corner,' he said, pointing to a table where four women sat.

'Sure. Fine. Okay, Anna?'

'No worries.'

The young kiltie looked at me. 'You Australian?'

'Too right,' I answered.

'Me too,' he said and threw his head back laughing as he guided us through the tables to our seats.

It turned out that the group of two mothers and two daughters lived locally. They were having their annual girlie night out. I was nearly blinded by the bling around their necks, wrists and fingers.

After a long toing and froing about the menu, we opted for a traditional Scottish dinner of steak pie with mashed potatoes, served with neeps and haggis.

When the meal arrived, I blanched at the colour and bulk of it. 'Mum never cooked anything like this,' I whispered to Fiona.

'Me neither, but it'll be a change from curry,' she giggled.

The meat pie wasn't too bad, full of flavour and topped with light puff pastry. I noticed that Fiona pushed the neeps and haggis to the side of her plate and I copied her.

When we'd reached the coffee stage, staff pushed back tables from a polished floor area about six square metres in front our table. A drum roll announced the appearance of two young girls I judged to be in early teens and a boy about sixteen. They were dressed in kilts and beautiful smiles lit up their faces.

'Does everyone in Scotland have great complexions?' I asked Fiona.

'It's the rain that keeps their skin soft, Anna,' she retorted.

For the next half hour the dancers swirled and dipped with grace and energy, smiling as they moved through complicated jigs and reels.

Fiona, beside me, swayed her shoulders from side to side, rippling her fingers along the edge of the table as if it was piano keys. At one point she yelled in my ear, 'Ye enjoyin' yourself, Anna?'

All I could do was nod. When the music stopped and the dancers left to deafening applause, I asked Fiona if she was ready to leave.

'My goodness, Anna, we'll be here for a while yet. The entertainment has only started. We have to stay for a bit o' craic.' She looked at her watch. 'It's only ten o'clock!'

I wanted to get back to Kate's. The name scrawled on a dusty box was all I could think of. I wanted to tell Fiona about finding it but, at the same time, I wanted to be alone when I opened it. My quandary was solved by the wail of bagpipes as a troop of pipers appeared from each side of the stage. Then I remembered something my mother used to say: 'Be with the person you're with and enjoy the moment.' The box could wait another little while.

As the night wore on, the entertainment became a mixture of music, comedians telling funny stories and still more music and dancing. No one wanted to dance with Fiona, so she just danced herself around the tables, singing her heart out. She knew the lyrics of every song and eventually the young Australian waiter invited her up to the stage to sing with him. Their voices blended so neatly you'd think they'd been rehearsing for weeks.

Over two hours later, Fiona was saying cheerio and vowing undying friendship to the women at our table. With a bit of coaxing from me, we set off for our lodgings.

'My oh my, Anna, wasn't that young man gorgeous? Wish I was

twenty years younger.' She took her high-heeled shoes off, sang at top of her lungs about 'Highland glens, bracken bens' and other place names I couldn't make out. She marched along in front of me and the gap between us got longer. When she reached the gate, she called out to me, 'Don't ye know 'The Hiking Song', Anna?'

I just shrugged. 'No.'

'Och, never mind, I'll sing it tae ye on the way home. I'm away to bed. See you in the mornin'.'

'Goodnight, Fiona. Thanks for the good time and thanks for coming to Oban with me.'

'No worries,' she said laughing and moved inside.

I sat on one of the wicker chairs and let the soft cool air and the scent of the sea surround me.

# 51

I woke up early next morning feeling like I'd been tortured in some way. My neck and back hurt and I could hardly lift my arms. Fiona's snores sounded like they'd lift the roof. I heaved myself out of bed, threw a jumper on over my pyjamas and went out to the shed.

When I pulled the box down from the shelf, grey dust billowed around my face, blinding me and making me sneeze. I carried it carefully as if it held pieces of Waterford Crystal, and took it to the table at the front of the house. Fiona still snored.

I dusted the box and scrubbed my hands clean before peeling tape from the opening. Inside: A parcel wrapped in blue tissue paper on top of some notebooks and a couple of dog-eared diaries.

Two little baby jackets, one white, one pale yellow with bootees and hats to match, lay snuggled together. Beneath this bundle a small white knitted blanket embroidered with roses and forget-me-nots. No tags or notes to tell me more about them. Nothing. I fondled them, smelled them, stared at them. Then wrapped them up and laid the parcel aside.

The jotters were labelled and dated. I spread them out before me. I had the feeling that they were daring me to open them. The only sound from inside the house was Fiona – still snoring.

**52**

I gingerly opened the notebook dated Glenhill 1963. Mum's handwriting leapt from the page. I flicked through it hoping that words about the feud between my mother and grandmother would leap out at me. It seemed to be mainly filled with Mum's prattling about school and friends and how her mother kept telling her off for not doing chores. When I spotted my father's name I started to read:

### *15 August 1963 – Glenhill*

*I am so excited. I met a terrific-looking boy in Dunoon today. He's over six feet tall. Black hair. Dark eyes and gorgeous smile. His name is Peter. He's from Newcastle and says 'loove', not 'love'. But I like how he says my name. El…ean…or. When most people say my name, it comes out 'Elner'.*

*Peter and I met on the foreshore after the protest march. We met again on the ferry.*

*I was standing alone at the stern enjoying the view when I felt someone stop beside me. I knew it was Peter before I turned to see him and before he spoke. He asked me if he could get me a drink or something to eat, but just then Fiona arrived balancing two cups of tea and a plate of biscuits. We found a seat and Peter and I wagged our chins and flirted for the rest of the journey. He asked me what I'd like to do with my life. No one has ever asked me that before. I told him I'd like to get on one of the big ships that sailed the waters beyond this stretch of sea and sail over the horizon to some place like Singapore or Sydney.*

*Fiona wandered off. I guess sick of our drooling at each other.*

*In spite of my stilettos, Peter stood tall above me. His hands on the rail looked strong. I think his fingers would be comfortable strumming a guitar or holding a scalpel.*

*What do I like about him?*

*The way he stands tall and confident.*

*The way he holds his head when concentrating.*

*He asks questions about my life.*

*The sharp clean look in his eyes.*

*His smile. His smile. His smile!*

*While the boat docked, we talked about the scenery, my (hated) job in the village drapers shop. He asked if I had brothers or sisters and what kind of house we lived in. He asked if I'd mind if he wrote to me. I asked him why and he said he wanted to keep in touch. He's in a hiking club and he will be back in Scotland for a tramp through the Western Highlands in two weeks time. I watched him write my address and wondered what kind of things he'd say in a letter. I could hear my heart pounding like it was about to burst through my ribcage and my hands were sweaty. We lingered on the dockside, looking at each other's eyes each not wanting to be the one to break contact. I wonder what my mother will say when I get a letter from England.*

## 10 September 1963

*Since the trip to Dunoon, I've thought a lot about Peter and wonder if he's got a new job, or a new girlfriend. I've been racing home each day to check the post, hoping he'll honour his promise to write to me. So far – nothing. I'll probably never hear from him again. It's so boring around here.*

## 30 September 1963

*Fiona and I went to the pictures to see Natalie Wood in* West Side Story. *Still haven't heard from Peter.*

## 16 October 1963

*At last. A letter. He wanted to see me when he did the Western Highlands walk but the schedule didn't allow any free time. He tried to picture me in hiking boots and outsize mac huddled into a hilltop with drops of rain*

126

*sticking to my hair. He enjoyed our short time together and remembers the fun we had on the ferry. He likes my hair.*

*He's got a new job – a junior management position – and the company are paying for him to study accounting. He's looking for digs and he'll send me his address when he writes to me again. My first letter. I liked it. I've read it ten times. It was like he was speaking to me. I could hear the softness of his voice in the words. Fiona begged me to let her read it but I wanted it to be all mine. I didn't want the words to lose some of their magic by anybody else touching them. (I feel bad about that but Fiona understands.)*

### 29 October 1963

*Letter number two came today with a return address. I wrote straight back to him. This is the first letter I've written to a boy and I didn't know what to say so I told him about the time Fiona and I nearly went to America.*

### 16 November 1963

*Letter number 3.*

*Peter apologised for not writing sooner. He's studying for exams at night school. I'll probably not hear from him for a while. I've put the letter with the others in my bottom drawer under my pyjamas.*

### 21 December 1963

*A Christmas card came today from Peter wishing me all the best for the New Year. He liked the things I said in my letter. I feel sorry for him not having family at Christmas. I bought a Christmas card and a birthday card for him. Must ask him when his birthday is.*

### 14 February 1964

*Today I got a valentine card postmarked Newcastle. I can't believe it. It was in a white box tied with red ribbon. It's got hearts with arrows through*

*them and the front cover is white satin with pink and white roses. It doesn't
have a signature but it is Peter's handwriting.*

*My mother started to open it before I could get to it but I pulled the
packet from her and ran across to show it to Fiona. She was really impressed.
When I came back I hid it in my bottom drawer. I will keep it forever. Mum
asked me if he was a Catholic (I knew she'd ask that). I told her I didn't
know, I hadn't asked him, and she ranted on about no daughter of hers will
marry outside the church. I ignored her and I've been in my room since. He
hasn't even asked me to marry him yet but I think if he did I'd say yes.*

The valentine card…the one in the old rusty suitcase…the one Mardi
and I giggled over! Why hadn't Mum and I giggled over it?

## 20 February 1964

*Mum's on a campaign to get me to go out with some of the local boys. She
says that John Ferguson is a nice boy and wants to go out with me. I told
her if he doesn't have the gumption to say that to my face I won't go out
with him. Anyway, I can't stand him.*

## 7 March 1964

*I haven't heard from Peter in ages and I've agreed to go to the pictures with
Frank Welsh. He's good-looking and he's a good dancer but I don't trust
him. Fiona says she heard that he's a bit pushy when it comes to saying
goodnight. He's the head altar boy at St Conval's – Mum thinks she's won
the coupon. Fiona's going with Jimmy Bogle. The four of us are going to the
St Patrick's night dance together.*

## 17 March 1964

*Disaster.*

*I will never tell a soul (other than Fiona) what the head altar boy did
to me. My hands can hardly hold this pen. I don't know how to describe
what happened. I don't remember ever feeling so terrified.*

*I don't know what to do.*

*What to think.*

*What to say.*

*The smell of him is still in my nose. Why did I let him convince me to leave while everyone else was dancing and having a good time?*

*He coaxed me round to the back of the church hall. It was dark as pitch and our shoes squelched on the peaty ground. He pulled me forward to a dry corner under the dyke.*

*I can see myself being led blindly through the darkness while the dance music got fainter. When we reached the dry patch, the only sound I heard was his heavy breathing. He turned round, grabbed my arms and forced me to the ground. I tried to fight him off but I had no defence against his weight. (Who will ever believe that?) He started tearing at my clothes.*

*Savagery.*

*Brute force.*

*Violation.*

*Repugnance.*

*Disgust.*

*Mild words compared to how I feel.*

*The thought of being seen or heard by people in the hall terrorised me. Without a word, he pummelled and thrust his way into me. He snorted and slavered until he'd finished, then hung over me like a hunk of sweaty meat covered in whisky-smelling breath. The last thing I saw as I scrambled away from him was the orange tip of his cigarette, glowing and still, in the dark. I climbed the embankment over the bridge and ran onto the road.*

*Fear made me run. Fear of my degradation being noticed gave me energy that I never knew I had. Fear that I will be judged guilty by anyone who hears about what he did to me.*

*I ran to Fiona's place. She recognised my need to keep the truth of things secret. Thank God for Fiona.*

## 53

I went back to the beginning of this entry and read through it again.

One more undated entry had two words in thick, black ink. 'I'm pregnant!'

I put the book down. Picked it up again. Flicked back through the pages I'd just read. Fanned the following pages. Nothing. I sat and stared at the words.

Why? Why didn't she tell me about this?

Just then Fiona called out from the doorway, 'Mornin'. Anna. Have ye had breakfast?' Her feet were bare and she'd wrapped herself in a big blanket. Frizzy spikes of hair almost hid her face and the rims of her eyes were black tinged with blue.

'Not yet…been too busy. You'll never guess what I've found.'

She came and sat beside me. 'What've ye got? Show me.'

I showed her the parcel and the books. 'More of Mum's diaries.'

'Well now, would ye believe that!'

'I knew she'd have written more.' I reached for the parcel of baby things. 'Look what else I found.'

She peeled of the tissue paper and stared long and hard at the contents. 'Well I never! Imagine this still bein' here after a' these years.' She fondled the tiny hats. 'Look at the stitchin' in these. I bet Kate parcelled them up afore Ellie came home from hospital. She prob'ly packed the notebooks away when she realised She and Peter were no' comin' back.'

'You know, Fiona, once, before she'd gone into hospital, I went into her room to watch her while she slept. I lay beside her and brushed wisps of hair away from her face. I thought that if I was dying I'd want to endow something of value to the people I loved. Now, reading this,

I finally have her legacy. This is her truth. I understand now that she sheltered me from the hurt and bigotry of her girlhood. These tiny clothes and her writings have placed her firmly here in Oban. Imagine. She made these. Why did she never tell me about this?'

Fiona re-wrapped the parcel and picked up the notebooks. 'Tell ye what, Anna, I'll get us some tea and toast an' ye can tell me all about it while we eat. Maybe after breakfast, we'll go for a wee jaunt aroun' the Highlands. I think that'll do ye the world of good.'

She moved away. I carried on reading.

## 25 April 1964 – Glenhill

*I'm pregnant and my mother hates me.*

*No one understands the revulsion I feel for Frank Welsh, and for myself. I want to shed my skin and become something or someone else – what freedom I'd find in that. Mostly, I stay in my room, coming out only for meals. It's like being in a house of mourning. Mum appeals to her full list of saints to rescue me from a life of disgrace. She doesn't ask about my pain or how I feel. I think she enjoys my misery. At mealtimes she slaps dishes of food on the table and I can almost taste the bitterness fermenting in her heart. I can't talk to her about pregnancy or about the child that is growing inside me.*

*Fiona says I should write a list of the questions that are bombarding my brain, and leave it by Mum's chair side, but I know it will lead to further rejection. I want to ask her why I feel so sick every morning and why I am so tired.*

*Yesterday morning, after a particularly bad bout of vomiting, when she was cleaning her collection of brass ornaments, I asked her to make an appointment with Doctor Kinloch. She said, in a voice made of stone, 'You got yourself into this mess and seeing a doctor won't help. You'd be better off seeing a priest.'*

*Dad heard her and asked, 'What earthly good would a priest dae?'*

*'For one thing, he'd convince your daughter that she should marry Frank Welsh,' Mum said, spitting the words the way a snake spits venom.*

## 26 April 1964

*I'd never seen Dad angry or heard him talk to my mother the way he did yesterday. He said to her that for once in her life she should think about me. That I needed their help and advice. He told her that he knows Frank Welsh and it would be a sad and lonely life for me if I were to marry him. He stared at Mum as though she was some kind of monster. I think he suspects what happened.*

*Mum said nothing but her polishing got faster and faster and the thumps on the table as she put ornaments down, got louder and louder. When she eventually stopped, the three of us were silent like a tableau on a stage. Mum sat still and stared out the window. The duster lay limp in her lap, as if it too, was exhausted.*

*Me and Dad stood in the middle of the floor looking like we were waiting for some miracle to happen. Then she stared at me with a hatred so powerful it made me cringe. I want to take a chisel and mallet to the stone of her reserve… chip away at it until it cracks. Why can't she see my pain? I feel so old. My worries are about old people things. I can't believe, that six weeks ago the only thing I thought about was my hair, what I'd wear going out, and Peter.*

## 27 April 1964

*Grumpy Stevenson, my boss in the draper's shop, knocked on our door today demanding to know when I was coming back to work. I heard Dad talking to him but didn't hear what was said. I believe people standing around on the oval are whispering about me. Old Ashwood has probably grasped the gossip with both ears and spilled it out his mouth to anyone who'll listen. My days of laughter and adventure are ended and I am floating along on a wave of degradation. Some nights I lie awake while anguish sits in my throat like a ball that refuses to move.*

*Last night, I smashed every one of my records into smithereens — didn't even look at the sleeves — tore them up in shreds and carted the lot out to the bin. No more dancing to the Beach Boys music in front of the mirror with Fiona — she'll be furious.*

## 28 April 1964

*My dad supports my decision not to marry, but I have to leave the village to spare my mother the sight of her wayward daughter. He's arranged for me to live with his sister Kate in Oban during the waiting time. Dad keeps looking at me — I think he wants me to tell him what happened — how can I tell this gentle man that I've been brutalised. Trying to talk about it to anyone causes my throat to jamb up and I feel the pain all over again.*

## 29 April 1964

*Feelings of misery and confusion are growing like a fungus in my mind. Early this morning, before anyone was awake, I walked the country roads around the village. I saw new birth in the bushes and plants. At one spot, I saw a robin tweeting and fluffing on a wire fence where raindrops sat on the barbs. It looked so free — freer than I can ever be now. That tiny life seemed so much more important than mine. I feel less than a robin on a barbed-wire fence. For a moment I saw the bird as an expression of love and I floated like a fish in water, flying without wings. Then ugly faces emerged to render me and the world around me into grotesque forms.*

*I don't care what I look like. I haven't washed my hair for a week. My clothes hang like bags on me but I suppose that will change soon.*

*Fiona came over today and we sat on my bed and sobbed. It's like both of us are in trouble.*

*She kept wringing her hands and brushing her hair away from her face and every few minutes, she asked, 'What're ye gonna do, Ellie?'*

*I've written to Peter telling him all about it. It breaks my heart knowing that he knows the truth about my situation and that I'll soon be leaving home. I sent him a book of poems to thank him for his kindness and friendship and so that he'd remember me. The year that was to be the best of my life is off to a bitter start — bitter as the winds that blow outdoors.*

## 30 April 1964 – Glenhill

*Saying goodbye to Fiona was really hard. She said she'll visit when she can.*

*We both cried like babies. I told her I'd be all right with Aunt Kate. We hugged each other and I watched her trail across the road with her head bowed.*

That was the last entry. I picked up notebook 3.

## *1 May 1964 – Oban*

*I do like Aunt Kate. She's a roly-poly kindly soul who smells of lavender and wears lovely hats when she goes out of doors. Her cottage is a haven of comfort. Shining white lace under panels of soft pastel shades dress the windows. Fat floral cushions are scattered here and there on comfy upholstered furniture, and ceramic figurines sit on lace doilies to decorate dark wood dressers and tables.*

*A photo of a man in military uniform sits at an angle on the mantelpiece. In all my visits here, I'd never paid much attention to it. While we were enjoying our first cup of tea together, I asked Kate about it. 'That's Joseph, my husband,' she said, with a wistful smile. She told me that Joseph had gone to war in 1942 and never came back. They'd only been married a few weeks. I asked her why she'd never married again and she said, 'Oh well now, I did get some offers but I refused to settle for less than the best. Joe was the best.' Now I know I was right about Frank Welsh.*

*My bedroom here is smaller than my room at home but it has lots of drawers and cupboards for my things. The walls and doors are painted white. The bedspread, and the giant pillows on top of it, is made with heavy white cotton that has sprigs of sky-blue forget-me-nots printed at random on it. No lace lies against the windows in this room, but two long sateen drapes match exactly the blue on the bedspread. When I wake each morning, I open them wide then hop back into bed to look out at a garden much like Dad's. A little vegetable patch is separated from a herb garden by a trellised archway where roses are just about to burst into bloom. From the tiny bit of colour I can see on the buds, I think they will be yellow.*

*It feels good to be away from Mum and her staring and praying and fury.*

What would Mum think of the state of the house she described? The blue curtains now grey, the white paint yellowed and chipped? The bedrooms smelled of dust and old sweat. The lovely bed linen Mum had described had been replaced with rolled-up sleeping bags at the end of each bed.

## 3 May 1964

*Today, Kate and I planted rose bushes along her driveway. Getting my hands into fresh-turned soil reminded me of Dad.*

*I no longer feel sick in the mornings and being here with Kate, is helping me push the horror of St Patrick's night far back into my mind.*

## May 4th 1964

*After breakfast we walked for miles amongst the hills, and in the afternoon, we knitted bootees and started on baby jackets. Kate has plans to make tiny blankets trimmed with satin. In spite of my anger for the way I got pregnant, my feelings for this little person growing in me are beginning to change. Is it possible I could love this baby? I don't know if this is how I'm supposed to feel right now but I'm not going to worry about it.*

*Kate borrowed books from the local library about childbirth and looking after babies and I'm ploughing my way through them. I want to learn as much as I can about the process. By midsummer the baby will be kicking and moving inside me. I wonder what that will feel like.*

## May 5th 1964

*Dad and Fiona came to visit but the disgrace was too much for Mum. According to Dad, she's still praying for the salvation of my soul. For the first time in ages, Fiona and I didn't cry. She has started going out regularly with Jimmy Bogle and she looks happy. She's now in training to be a nurse. I wonder how she'll go with the smells of blood and vomit.*

## 54

### *6 May 1964*

*When Kate and I came back from shopping today, a car was parked in the driveway. Andy and his wife, Anne Marie, had brought their first-born daughter to meet me. It's the first time I've heard from either of my brothers since this all happened. I felt relieved when I saw their smiles. They hugged me and asked how I was feeling. They brought me a tiny white cotton nightgown for the baby and a little globe of the world. The globe is a gift from Jack, who is in England playing cricket. Andy said it's to help me find the right direction on my journey through life. We spent the afternoon talking about babies. I wanted to ask Andy about Mum but it would've spoiled a pleasant time and, anyway, he never mentioned her. They left Kate and me, waving and wishing us well. I feel hopeful now. With Kate's care I will get through this time.*

### *7 May 1964*

*A letter came from Peter today. It doesn't seem to matter to him that I'm carrying another man's baby. He says he wants me to keep writing to him — his feelings are stronger than friendship and he sends me his love. He wrote, 'Much love to a beautiful person who is my friend.' I can't believe he hasn't rejected me. I am hoping that his words are the beginning of a journey to a place in his life and a kinder world. He enclosed photos that he'd taken while hiking in the Highlands. They were wrapped in a soft silk scarf. I will keep the scarf around my neck and the letter under my pillow.*

### *8 May 1964*

*Kate's house sits in the middle of Longsdale Road, which tapers off where the path to McCaig's Folly begins. This is supposed to be a replica of the Colosseum in Rome and it is one of my favourite spots in Oban. When I was very young, and Dad and I visited Kate, we'd climb to the top, and when I complained of sore legs, he'd give me a piggyback the rest of the way. Tomorrow Kate and I plan on tackling the climb to the top. We'll sit at Pulpit Hill and look across to the Isle of Mull and watch the steamers churn along the Firth of Lorne.*

## 14 May 1964

*Kate brought me home from hospital today. I have lost the baby. I remember sitting on a bench watching the sea and talking to Kate about knitting patterns. The scent of rhododendrons and wild irises lining the pathway was all around us. We decided it was time for a cup of tea and started down the slope. My foot slipped on blossoms that had fallen from the bushes. I remember trying to grasp a branch but it was wet and slithered through my fingers like an oily rope. I heard Kate say 'Mind your step, Eleanor' just before I fell.*

*What happened after that is a blur of voices, a car engine running, bumps and sways and pain like a white hot knife cutting into me and Kate saying, 'Hush, darling, hush. You're going to be fine.' I woke up in a hospital bed with Kate holding my hand and crooning some ancient Gaelic song that I'd never heard before.*

*A doctor came in and said, 'You are no longer pregnant, Eleanor.' It was as if he was telling me the time of day. Then he left me to absorb that bit of information. I think he has judged me to be worthless – like Mum and Father O'Malley. Kate is nursing my bruises, my broken arm and my battered heart. She has written to my father.*

## 18 May 1964

*Dad came today to beg me to come home with him. He said my job is waiting for me and Fiona misses me, but those things don't concern me. I told him about how I felt about Peter and that Peter had written to me.*

*When he asked me what I wanted to do, I told him I need more time here. Dad said, 'I'll miss ye, Ellie,' and left. I feel sorry for him. I watched his shoulders stoop as he walked down the path. I will miss my dad. I nearly ran after him, but I'm glad I didn't.*

*Before going to bed, I wrote to Peter. I told him it would be better if he forgot all about me.*

## 19 May 1964

*I feel like I'm moving around in someone else's dream. My thoughts are as clouded as the flowers hiding in the Highland mist and I spend a lot of time staring into space, not looking at anything, not wanting anything.*

## 8 June 1964

*This morning as I walked along the harbour wall, I heard a voice call my name. I turned into the breeze and saw Peter striding across the road with his arms spread in greeting. I couldn't believe it. He stood a few feet away from me and said, 'Recognised the gorgeous hair.' I stood dumbstruck. He came towards me and folded me into his arms. He smelled like fresh air and heather. We stayed like that for a long time before I took his hands. We kissed…the sweetest, warmest kiss. I stroked the outline of his jaw and buried my face in his chest to listen to his heartbeat.*

*We will stay in Oban until I'm fully recovered. He has found us a place to live and says we will be together for the rest of our lives. I am overjoyed. He told me he'd come to take me home. It was all he needed to say.*

## 15 June 1964

*When Peter touches me, I seem to live in every inch of my being. I can feel something sizzle in my veins. I can't get enough of his hands on my body. He envelopes me in a tenderness that flows over me, over the rooms we share, on the Streets we walk and the hills that we climb. Everything feels strange and full of wonder. With Peter beside me, tall and strong in the summer sun and clean sea air of Oban, it is as if nothing bad has ever happened to me. Through Peter I can feel myself becoming whole again. We are making plans for a future together.*

## 16 June 1964

*It seems to me that the pain I have suffered has led me to a light that comes from Peter and from the love that blesses our togetherness. He wants me to make peace with my mother. He said, out of the blue today, 'I think you should go and see her, and try again to make amends for the things you have said to each other.' For his sake, and because family is important to him, I have agreed. But I've warned him that the dimple on his chin will not make her accept him. The fact that we are living in sin, as she will say we are, will really stick in her throat. We are going tomorrow. It will be good to see Fiona.*

## 17 June 1964

*What a shambles. She'll never accept Peter. She'll never know how wonderful he is.*

<h1 style="text-align:center">55</h1>

I could hear faint sounds of water running, dishes clinking and Fiona singing softly in the kitchen. I put the journal down and closed my eyes and tried to see how it had been for Mum. Seeing my grandmother and talking with her in her old age, I couldn't believe she could be cruel. Then I recalled that I'd read something in Mum's last diary about 'a wall keeps us from seeing the truth of each other'.

Fiona arrived with a tray and started putting cups and teapot on the table. She sat beside me. I carried on reading.

Mum's description of 'shining white lace and panels of soft pastel shades at the windows' denied the reality of the state of the house as I saw it now.

'This house is so different from how Mum described it, Fiona.'

'Well now, Anna, Ellie was describing something as it was ower forty years ago. 'Member, Kate's been dead these twenty years and this wee house has had nothing but transient holiday makers in it since then.'

'Mmmm, I know.'

I asked Fiona if she thought I should take the notebooks back so that Gran and Grandpa could read them.

'Och, I'm sure I don't know the answer tae that one, Anna. Mibbe it's a case of sleeping dogs. Then again, mibbe they'd want to ken how things were in your mother's heart at the time. Let's mull it over for a bit. In my estimation, they might find it all too hard to face the truth of it seein' as they're in their last years o' livin'.'

'Did you ever talk to them about Mum's predicament?'

'Well, no. At first I was too henny tae go near them. But a while after Elner an' Peter left an' your grandpa had just come back from a weekend at Kate's, your gran met me in the street one day. "How are you, Fiona?" she asked. I was so surprised, I nearly fell off my stilettoes. After that, now and again, she'd invite me ower for a cup of tea. But by then me an' Jimmy were too busy getting' tae know each other. But I dae think your gran had finally come to an understandin' of what your mother had gone through and realised that Elner wasn't coming back.' As she said this, Fiona yawned.

# 56

Before heading north to Fort William, we walked to the local shops for lunch.

Fiona pointed out the house that Mum and Dad had lived in before they left Scotland.

'Did you visit them while they stayed in this house?' I asked.

'No, Anna, I only ever met them at Kate's.'

I heard a faint sound of music coming through the open front door. 'Can you hear a pipe band, Fiona?'

'Must be your imagination.'

The sound got louder. I grabbed my camera and shot through the door. What a spectacle! It was the local band on a fund-raising stint. It paraded from a nearby school yard along the harbour wall and stopped in the town centre. For the next hour, I lost myself in the colour and sound of the spectacle. I never noticed the point when my feet started tapping to the birr and smeddum of the pipes.

<h1 style="text-align:center">57</h1>

Early next morning while Fiona was still asleep, I climbed a hundred and fifty steps to a bench that sits on Pulpit Hill, near McCaig's Folly. The rhododendron bushes were bowed down with blossom and I could see bees darting amongst the petals. I watched passenger ferries, with flags waving, and two small cutters with sails full blown making furrows on the water. I thought about Kate and Mum so many years ago talking about babies. I wanted to hold this time of solitude close to me always.

On the way down, I looked at each step. Was this the one Mum skidded on? Or this one? Was that gouge made by the heel of my mother's shoe?

I walked along the harbour wall and imagined I could see young lovers meeting and embracing. I tried to grasp the essence of Mum and Dad as I moved around the streets but distance and time held it back from me. The feeling reminded me of the time after Mum's funeral when other mourners had gone and no one was around to talk to. I'd sit in her chair and read or I'd talk to the walls.

At breakfast, when Fiona found me staring into space she asked what was on my mind.

'I don't know if I can put it into words, Fiona. It's like I've lost the scent of Mum here. I can't pick up any signs that she ever lived here. I thought maybe by coming here I could touch her life, maybe get closer to her.'

Fiona looked at me and gave a loud long sigh. Her shoulders drooped and her body sagged. 'I've got no cure for what's ailin' you, love,' she said, and asked me to tell her more about Mum's last days.

I told Fiona how over the years I used to massage Mum's feet at the end of a busy day and we'd joke about the differences between her long thin toes and my stubby digits.

'On the morning of the day she died, I sang to her while giving her a manicure. I sat by her bed and watched her face and thought about the times before she'd gone into hospital, when she'd waken in the night and I'd lie beside her. It would be quiet, like before dawn in our garden. I'd see her looking almost normal and believe that she wasn't dying, that it was a lie created by our fears.

'The night she died, she didn't know I was beside her. It was a Sunday evening just on dusk. Only me and a nurse beside her. I remember holding her hand and trying to hear her breathe when the nurse told me she was gone. That was it. I expected a noise of some kind. A drumbeat. A declaration to mark her passing. Only my heart beat and the sound of the nurse attending to wires and plugs around the bed cancelled complete silence. I waited and waited thinking that they'd made a mistake.

'After a long, long time, I heard a voice. I think it was a doctor saying, "Excuse me, Anna, can I call someone for you? Do you need transport home?" I said nothing, just sat twisting my hands around my scarf and looking at the dead monitor. Finally, a nurse escorted me to a little room and made me a drink of something. I don't remember what. When she left, I walked home, phoned our neighbour, Mrs Daly, and my friend Mardi. I think I wept for weeks. I didn't know what to do. Mum had left detailed instructions about the service and Mrs Daly made the necessary phone calls.'

I looked sideways at Fiona and saw tears sitting at the corner of her eyes as if they were waiting for me to turn away before they'd trickle down her cheeks.

'It must have been very hard for you bein' on your own like that,' she said.

'Yes it was, but, it's like, I don't know... I miss her more here. It's been great hearing the things you've told me about Mum and reading her diaries. Those two things have made her partly come alive for me. I can't thank you enough for that but...'

'No need to thank me, Anna. Just try and be as happy as you can be, that'll be thanks enough.'

'I know her feet walked these streets and she laughed and cried and sang here, but I can't see her. Same as it is when I'm at my grandparents looking around, it's like I've lost her again.'

'Well, ye see, Anna, your memories of your mother are back in Australia. It's only people like me an' your grandparents that connect Ellie to the places aroun' here.'

We had another cup of tea then filled the rest of the morning in by shopping in the main street. I bought an Arran jumper for Joe to keep him warm on field trips. For Mrs Daly, a set of tartan mugs which the shop parcelled and freighted to Adelaide. For Mardi I chose a tartan car rug, and for Augie, Argyll socks.

When we started back to Glenhill, I asked Fiona if she wanted the radio on.

'Not yet. I've been thinking about a time when your mam tried to convert some of the non-Catholic weans in the street. I'll tell you an' it will give you an inklin' about the bigotry that existed at that time – in some cases, it still does.'

'Hope we'll have enough time before we get back to Glenhill.'

'Sure we will. I can make a story as long or as short as we need it.'

## 58

Fiona reached under her seat, pulled a lever and let the seat collapse back. She closed her eyes and started talking.

'We were seven years old and preparin' for our first communion. Your Mam felt sorry for some Protestant weans that lived in our street. She believed that they'd die with the stain of original sin on their souls so she took the matter into her own hands. Just after school one day, she stood on the top step at the front door of your grandparent's house, with a white lace curtain draped around her shoulders. She had your gran's Roman Missal open in her hands. Three Gibson girls and two McCubbins sat cross-legged on the lawn in front of her. I stood beside her. I think I was supposed to be the altar boy.'

I'd never heard this story until now, and when Fiona laughed at an image only she could see, I had the feeling she'd made the whole thing up purely for the fun of it.

'Your mam had just started to say the introduction to the Mass in Latin. She droned "Introibo ad altare Dei" tryin' to sound seriously Catholic an' holdin' her right hand up like a priest giving a blessing. 'The McCubbins were only about three or four at the time an' they looked at your mam as if she was nuts an' started fidgetin'. She glared at them an' said, "That means, I will go into the altar of God."

'She'd just finished speakin' when your gran came around from the backyard where she'd been hangin' out the washin'. The laundry basket landed at Ellie's feet an' your gran pulled the Missal from her hands. The curtain fell to the ground an' the students ran like the wind away from the wrath of your grandma, who started yellin' something about sharing the holy book with those people. I ran home an' hid behind the curtains in our living room.

'The next thing I saw was your gran takin' Ellie by the hand in a hurry. I learned later that she'd been taken to Father O'Malley for a lecture an' it took him ages to calm your gran down. He told her that convertin' people to the faith wasn't such a bad thing, an' that maybe your mam had a vocation to be a missionary. I think that might have been the beginnin' of the end of your mother's faith in the church.'

I asked Fiona what Grandpa said about all this.

'Well, knowin' the kind of man he is, he'd likely shrug his shoulders, take his gardenin' cap off a hook on the kitchen door an' saunter down to the hut for a quiet smoke.'

Fiona finished speaking, closed her eyes and slept the rest of the way home.

## 59

At Grandpa's birthday celebrations, Claire and her cousins buzzed around offering drinks and food to guests while others of the McCrae clan danced till their faces turned red and feet began to falter. I watched old and young join hands and weave their bodies through 'The Siege of Ennis'. Some dancers kicked off their shoes to skip through the movements and loud hand-claps beat time to the music of 'The Brown Jug Polka'.

Claire's hair was piled on top of her head with slides that sparkled in the light. The shine matched the long jangly sticks of silver hanging from her ears. She wore a short black crepe dress. High-heeled shoes were strapped to her feet with thin diamante bands. It looked like she knew everyone in the hall the way she moved around chatting to individuals and groups between dances.

She came over and sat with me for a few minutes, filling me in with some of the local gossip. She pointed to a spot where a group of young people stood. 'That's the McGlynn twins in the corner. The Cassidy boys are trying to catch their attention. Would you look at the silly buggers. Why don't they just go up and offer them a drink?' She said this softly with a hand up to her mouth.

'Maybe they're too shy.' I said.

'Shy, my arse! Vanity. That's the problem here. Their egos couldn't handle rejection.'

I laughed. 'D'you have a man in your life, Claire?'

'Nope. I lived with someone for two years. He's ten years older than me. We nearly got married a year ago but it all fell through at the last minute. We stayed together for a while but finally split on the fourteenth of May this year, at three o'clock in the afternoon. So now I'm single and celibate.'

'What happened?'

'Well, he wants to start a new life in Australia but I've a good job here. I don't want to leave my family and friends, so I said, bugger off. I miss him, though. I'm still not sure if I made the right decision. What about you? You seein' anyone?'

'The fella I fancy has been away a lot and I've been busy, so I'm not sure if it'll ever get off the ground.'

'Well, I wish you all the best. Hope you have better luck than me.'

'He'd love this party,' I said. 'He's rapt in things Celtic.'

'Well, if you ever come back to Scotland, bring him with you,' Claire said laughing. 'We'll have a repeat performance especially for the two of you.'

I loved the way everyone joined in the dancing. Three-year-olds danced with sixty-year-olds and teenagers danced with their parents.

Gerard saw me watching him and Sheena showing off their dancing skills to other young children and called out to me, 'G'day, Anna!'

Grandma sat at a little table in a corner, her good hand tapping out the beat of the music and her head moving from side to side. Two of the teens I'd met on my first day were sitting by her side, sharing a joke of some kind.

Fiona waved to me from across the room then came towards me. Her hair, shining with a deep chestnut glow, fell softly on her face and ended at the gold jewellery around her neck. Her wrists and fingers glinted, as if they were lights, against the blackness of her dress. She looked like she'd grown some inches since I'd last seen her.

I shuffled along the bench and she plopped down beside me.

'You look lovely, Fiona. Love your hair. The colour suits you.'

'Thanks, Anna. It's my Saturday night look. Had it done this afternoon. Isn't this a grand show for your grandpa? Hey listen, Anna, they're playing "The Dashing White Sergeant"! Come on, up ye' get.'

And with that she hauled me to my feet. Pretty soon I found myself in a group of eight people of varying ages and sizes. I'd no idea how to do the complicated movements. It seemed to me that for the next hour

I was pushed and pulled and prodded along a course of movements that everyone, except me, was completely at home with. Other dancers laughed at my clumsiness so the only thing to do was laugh with them. By the end of the dance, my shoes were under a bench somewhere, my jacket on a table and my hair looked liked it had been victimised by a gale-force wind. I felt exhilarated. Exhausted. Happy.

When the band took a break from playing, tin whistles appeared from pockets and fiddles and accordions were pulled from under seats. I'd never heard singing like it. It filled the rafters, bounced off the walls and filtered through to people filling plates with food in the side kitchen. They sang about partings; they sang about love; they sang about white crosses on roadside memorials. The smokers, gathered outside by the door, joined in choruses between puffs of nicotine.

Jack asked for quiet and introduced his eldest son to sing a solo for Grandpa. The strains of 'Dark Island' soared and floated with a clarity and beauty that made the hair on the back of my neck rise. Every note was perfect and clear like the water that flowed from the mountains to the river that ran through the village. Grandpa's eyes shone and he joined in the parts that his ageing vocal chords could manage. The words caused tears to well in my eyes for my absent mother. The last line of the song, 'that lovely dark island will be my last home', faded into the ceiling.

Andy's eldest granddaughter, Catherine, took Grandpa's arm and led him to the centre of the floor. The gathering made a circle around them and his faltering steps moved slowly to the tune of an old-time waltz. When the dance ended, everyone laughed at Grandpa's exaggerated bow to each corner of the room. Then, all joined hands and sang 'For He's a Jolly Good Fellow' so loud I was sure it could've been heard in Adelaide.

The ill feeling amongst my mother's family at the time of her defection to Australia had no apparent effect on this far-flung and extended web of connections.

When people started to leave, I helped Claire clean up bottles and cans and dishes. We walked home together over the stone bridge and onto the highway. Before going our separate ways home, we made plans for a pub crawl with her friends the next weekend.

## 60

We made up a group of seven chattering females. We sat amongst the noise of glass chinking against glass, and thumping on tables, at Finn Maccool's. A soccer match was showing on the TV – Celtic versus Aberdeen. The viewers roared as the players dribbled and feinted feet around the ball. The commentator's voice was lost amongst the music.

A tall blond man with a gorgeous smile stopped by our booth and said, 'Hello ,Claire. How're you doin'?'

Claire frowned, put her drink down slowly and turned to look at the voice. Someone giggled. Conversation around the table stopped. Claire's friends suddenly found interest in the TV screen, the coasters on the table top, the floor or the ceiling.

'Hi, Michael. I'm fine. How're you?' Claire said.

She and Michael looked at each other for what seemed like minutes, the way children focus on a forbidden jar of lollies. Michael licked his lips. He stood still. Claire's hands shook. They started to offer a hand to each other but pulled back like you would if you were about to touch a hot dish of something, then decided you needed the protection of oven mitts.

Defeated by the noise, they abandoned talking and Michael moved away to join the group watching TV.

Claire watched his back then grabbed her handbag and lunged towards the ladies. I followed her. We shut the door on the babble and clatter of the bar and moved to the far end of the washroom, where Claire grasped the edge of a washbasin with both hands and bent her head.

'What's the matter, Claire? You all right?'

'No, I'm not. I didn't expect to see him here.'

'Who is he?'

'He's Michael. The man I told you about.'

'The man you lived with?'

'Yup. He's the one. Michael bloody Welsh.'

I looked at Claire fighting back tears. She told me she hadn't seen him since they'd split. And while she said this, I thought, Welsh?… Welsh?

'Is he related to Frank Welsh?'

Claire looked at me. 'Yes. Michael's his son.'

The name clanged in my head like a clarion and I wish I'd paid more attention to him. Then words from my mother's diaries floated past me. 'Forced me to the ground. Thrusted. Hung over me.' I started to shake.

I couldn't look at Claire when I asked, 'D'you know his father?'

'I know he's an arrogant bastard – not fit to kiss Michael's feet. D'you know, when Michael and his brothers were little, their father used to beat them and lock them in cupboards if they didn't finish their dinner or if they made too much noise or if they got their sports clothes dirty. And Michael's mother was known to walk into doors or fall down stairs on a regular basis – like every time his father got drunk. That's the kind of man Frank Welsh was in his younger days.'

Claire's words soared over the thought that I'd just met the son of my mother's rapist. I felt like I was swimming in slime.

'His sons have had nothing to do with him for years. Michael can't stand knowing he walks the same streets as him, that's one of the reasons he wants to move to Australia.' She stopped talking and looked at me strangely. 'You look like you've seen a ghost. Why do you want to know about his father?'

I moved towards her and grabbed her arm. 'Listen to me, Claire. Michael is the son of the man who raped my mother and made her pregnant.'

She prised my fingers from her arm and stood back from me. 'What are you talking about? What did you just say?'

'I said, Frank Welsh raped my mother and got her pregnant.'

Claire jumped back from me as if I'd slapped her. 'So, was that the cause of the big conflict between her and Gran?'

'That's only the start of it. Because of him, my mum's life was a long hard journey. At least until she migrated to Australia.'

I told Claire what I knew and when I'd finished she said, 'I'm so sorry about what happened to your mother, Anna, but Michael is nothing like his father, he's the best person I know. He'd never harm anyone. We agreed not to see each other but that's no reflection on him. I'd like you to meet him, find out for yourself the kind of person he is.'

'Meet him? I couldn't…I'd…no way!'

Claire moved away and we stood at each end of the washroom. The bitterness of a time in my mother's life presented itself to me in this man's fair face. Bile rose to my throat. A parade of images swept across my eyes: Mum lying in a dark corner and pinned to the earth by a monster. Mum in a grey and spent body gasping her last breath thousands of miles from her homeland.

Hearing about Michael's suffering at the hands of his father, didn't soothe me and I told Claire, 'I want his father to suffer like my mother did. He has to pay for that injustice.'

'Maybe I'd feel such bitterness if it'd happened to my mother, but it's not Michael's sin,' Claire grumbled.

I asked her if she thought Michael knew what his father did to my mother. She stared at me and put her hands over her ears and closed her eyes like she wanted to shut the world out. She stayed like that for a minute.

Then she spat, 'How could he know about this? It happened before Michael or me or any one of us was born, and I can tell you this for nothing…no way would I burden Michael with this. I think it's time you left the past where it belongs, Anna. In the past.'

I shrank, like a sponge that'd just been squeezed.

Claire paced up and down and the only sound between us was the click of her heels on the black and white tiles. I saw the depth of her anger in her walk and the way she tossed her head back and glared at me.

She stopped in front of me. 'Listen, Anna, I know you're grieving for your mother, and you have a lot of healing to do. It vexes me to know what happened to her, but just as you can never walk in your mother's shoes, Michael could never, ever be his father. He doesn't deserve the hatred that you feel for his father to be put onto him.' She turned to face a mirror next to me and started flicking her fingers through her hair.

We stood looking at each other saying nothing. Claire's face took on a fierce and narrow look.

# 61

When we finally went back to the bar, I could see Michael's face in a mirror and suddenly the room was full of Michaels and I wanted to spit on each one of them. I realised I was being unreasonable. I also reminded myself that no one had given Mum cancer. Where could I put the blame for that?

We had one more drink then said goodbye to Claire's friends.

On the way home the silence in the car was so thick I could almost see it.

Suddenly Claire said, 'Michael has a heart the size of an elephant's.'

I looked at her. 'A heart as –'

She didn't let me finish. 'As soon as he was big enough, he used to get between his father and mother to protect her. And he'd make sure Arthur and Eddie, his siblings, were never again locked in a cupboard or beaten up. D'you know, Anna, when he was fourteen, he got a job. He saved every penny and by the time he was sixteen he had enough money to rent a house for the family. Except his father of course. That meant that, for the last few years of her life, his mother had peace and contentment she'd never known in her marriage. That's why I say his heart's as big as an elephant's.'

I tried to imagine a heart that big. 'Claire, how big do you think an elephant's heart is?'

She looked at me. She smiled. Next thing I knew we were giggling, then laughing, then I cried great gulping sobs that I couldn't stop. I cried until we reached Grandpa's.

Claire waited in the car with me until I calmed down. She offered me a box of tissues and said, 'You'll have your own thoughts about all of this, Anna. The stuff about your mother is new and your anger about her death is still raw. I understand that. I don't know what else to say to you except that if you don't want to meet Michael, I'll understand that too. But I want you to put that bad feeling out of your heart.'

'Maybe tomorrow.'

'No. Today. Right now. You let that feeling stay…it's like poison.'

She drove off. I went inside and shut the door.

I lay on top of my bed and thought about my mother. Then I began to search my conscience for the generous heart she'd believed I had, but all I found was rancour. I re-read the parts in her diary where she talked about the day Dad came to Oban and I thought about Fiona's version of the day she tried to reconcile with her mother.

I hardly slept all night.

## 62

I don't know what I expected to find in Scotland. Perhaps some things Mum hadn't told me about herself – photos of her childhood – friends she grew up with…something that would bring her alive again.

When I said all this to Grandpa the next morning, he looked at me puzzled. The way he tilted his head to the side reminded of Joe.

'Anna,' he said, cleaning his glasses, 'some questions hiv nae answers. I ken 'tis a terrible thing tae lose a parent when you're sae young, but it's jist as heartbreakin' for a parent tae outlive a child – nae matter how auld they are. Try no' tae ask why – it'll drive ye silly.'

I said nothing. No number of albums or talking about them could bring my parents back and I wondered why I came to be amongst so many strangers.

# 63

On my last Saturday in Glenhill, Grandma had gone off for a therapy session and Grandpa and I were sitting on a wooden bench in the garden, unravelling a twisted bunch of twine the size of a soccer ball. His old hands were picking slowly and gently at loose ends while I wound them around my fingers. He told me it would be a good idea to take myself away for the day.

When I asked why, he looked at me over the top of his glasses and said, 'It's the Orange Walk the day and usually that means trouble.'

'What d'you mean? What kind of trouble?'

'Well, it's like this. Each year on the Saturday nearest the twelfth of July, some Protestants still celebrate the Battle of the Boyne an' these streets come alive. It's nothin' but a crowd o' grown men an' the occasional woman, walkin' behind a band recallin' a battle fought in another country more than three hundred years ago. It angers and saddens me tae see sich behaviour.'

As he talked, words on the pages of books I'd read came alive. Phrases from Milton tumbled in my mind: religious climate of…unceasing disturbances…secular supremacy. I was struck by the notion that the zeitgeist of the seventeenth century still rang through this village.

'When I see them,' Grandpa went on, 'I think it must be hard work tae look sae furious for sae long.'

He finished talking and I was about to tell him about things Fiona and I had talked about, when Claire arrived.

'I see he's got you working already,' she said, laughing.

'Just passin' the time tellin' Anna aboot the twelfth an' keepin' our hands busy,' Grandpa said, tilting his hat to the back of his head. 'Where are you off tae the day?'

'Alice and Barb are waiting in the car. We're going for a drive to Ayr. Wanna join us, Anna?

'That's a grand idea, Claire,' Grandpa said. 'Be sure tae drive carefully now.' And to me he said, 'Go on, lass. You'll have a better time wi' Claire and her pals than sittin' here wi' the auld folk.'

# 64

I hadn't seen or heard from Claire since the night at Finn Maccool's but I'd thought a lot about what she'd said about Michael and leaving things in the past. The idea of being near the sea appealed to me. Things might become clearer.

'Thanks, Claire, I'd like that.' I picked up my bag and camera and said goodbye to Grandpa. We stowed our belongings into the boot of Claire's little red Pulsar, and set off with friendly smiles and chatty companionship:

'Lovely day for a drive.'

'Like the top you're wearing.'

'Enjoying your holiday?'

We piled into the car. I sat with Claire in the front.

We'd reached the end of the street when I heard the sound of marching music.

Claire pulled to the side of the road.

'This'll open your eyes, Anna,' Alice said, raising her eyebrows as if she'd asked a question.

The sound grew louder and a band appeared around the corner from Bridge Street.

They marched four abreast playing on flutes, whistles, horns and trombones. Orange and purple emblems on the drums matched bright sashes slung across dark suits of men wearing bowler hats. I could see small groups of people watching with tight lips and folded arms from doorways along the street. I noticed blinds being jerked down on nearby windows.

The music grew louder as they tramped towards St Conval's where, according to Claire, ten o'clock Mass was about to start. The band leader signalled a stop when he reached the last brick that marked the end of the church grounds. The ensemble turned so that their faces looked at the open door of the church. They marched on the spot while the bass drummer grinned and banged and stamped his feet. His efforts reduced the rest of the music to a whimper. Three bandsmen pocketed their tin whistles and separated themselves from the band to spit and jeer at the gates of the church.

I spied a group of altar boys in white albs slinking into a side door. Churchgoers with their eyes cast down tried desperately not to catch the attention of the hissing hangers-on by the roadside as they scurried through the gates.

The stench of hatred seeped out from the Orangemen and mixed with the angst of the congregation filing into the church. I shuddered at the strangeness of the world I found myself in.

I remembered the story Fiona had told me about Mum trying to convert non-Catholic children and realised that not much had changed in this village since then.

'It seems to me that the connection between generations has been wrought by a chain of intertwined histories and brutal events. Bigotry and hatred bred in a battle fought in 1690 has echoed down through the centuries to this village where people use it to create barriers and disrupt families.'

When I said this, Barb told me about her auntie Margaret, who'd braved the furore of her family and married the love of her life. Margaret was sixteen, her boyfriend was eighteen when they eloped.

'They got married in the side chapel of Paisley Abbey and his family would have nothing to do wi' Marg and her family hated him for taking her on a path of heresy – anyway, that's what my ma said.'

'What happened to them? Did they ever reconcile?'

'Nope, they got lodgings somewhere for a while but it was all too hard for them and they separated. After the divorce she married a nice Catholic boy who gave her a life of Hell 'cos she wasn't a virgin when she came to him. She's now a widow and an alcoholic who doesn't know one day from the next. My ma used to say, "None of us can help the things life has done to us but it's how we deal with those things that determine our characters" and obviously, Auntie Margaret didn't have what it took to make the experience work towards a good life – she chose to marry the first man who asked her.'

Everyone else in the car was silent and I thought about my mother and the courage it had taken to seek a new life in another country. Her bravery in standing up to the narrow-mindedness of her mother and the community that had bred her amazed me. I felt proud to be her daughter.

Barb asked me if we had parades like this in Adelaide.

'Depends what's happening – like sometimes trade unionists take to the streets in protest. And lately we've had marches against the treatment of refugees. But nothing like what we're seeing here. People at home tend to be tolerant about other folk's belief systems.'

Tension spread through the car.

'Can we just move on, Claire? I can't stand to see people behave like animals,' Alice said.

'Bloody morons,' Claire muttered and we set off for the coast.

# 65

As we sped along on the highway heading south, Claire asked, 'Anyone want music?'

'As long as it's something we can sing along to,' Barb said.

Claire slipped a CD into the slot. We rolled down the windows and sang 'I'm On My Way' at the top of our voices with the Proclaimers singing in the background. We sang to sheep grazing in fields and at people standing at bus stops in Irvine and Prestwick.

Smiles and frowns on faces whizzed past the car with each line of the song. We passed fields ringed with piles of stone built into walls that looked like it would take an earthquake to move them.

'This landscape is so different from where I live,' I said, as if I was talking to myself.

'What d'you mean?' – that was Alice.

'It's the distances between towns, and the greenness of the fields and the softness of the air.'

Claire asked, 'How long does it take you to get to the sea, Anna?'

'Depends on the weather. By bike it's fifteen minutes, by car three or four minutes.'

We were quiet for the rest of the trip.

**66**

The beach scenes at Ayr amused me. No bodies romped half-naked in the surf. No beach tents or sandcastles or giant towels draped over rocks. No flip-flops slapped the pavement. Couples on the promenade wore jeans and jackets, like their counterparts do in Rundle Mall. Young mothers paraded babies in shiny high prams decked out with fringed canopies and lace covers. The brown-feathered fat seagulls looked like they could do with a wash and a low-fat diet.

We stared out to sea for a few minutes before Claire grabbed my arm. 'Quick, Anna, we're gonna have a downpour.'

How could she know that? Was she psychic?

We made a beeline for one of the gazebos spaced along the lawns that separated the beach from traffic on the main street behind us. By the time we'd run a few yards to shelter, people had packed themselves undercover like sardines while madly pulling out plastic capes and bonnets from handbags and pram-bags. I could smell wet tweed. We huddled amongst the shoppers and toddlers and tourists while a grey slanting squall swept in from the sea. In less than ten minutes, as if sucked up by an enormous vacuum, it disappeared. The weather changed back again to summer and a double rainbow, as bright as any I'd ever seen, dipped into the horizon. The steam billowing from the pavement convinced me that the whole event hadn't been a hallucination.

We set off to find a good eating place, looking at menus posted on doors and windows until Barb suggested a place near the breakwater that served great seafood.

When we looked inside the Moorings, the waiters were almost running as they carried trays high above the heads of patrons and threaded their way around tables and chairs.

'Looks like we'd have a long wait here. Let's try somewhere else,' Claire said.

We'd just turned to leave when Barb pointed to a table in a far corner saying, 'Look, Claire. I think that's Michael and his pals.'

I stopped so quickly that Claire, behind me, nearly bowled me over onto a table.

She started to say something. When I turned to look at her, I couldn't quite work out the expression in her eyes. Was it a question? An apology? Anxiety? I didn't know and it didn't matter because the next thing I knew, one of Michael's friends spotted us and called us over.

Claire whispered to me as we moved towards them. 'I didn't plan this, Anna. I hadn't a clue that we'd bump into Michael. If you want to leave, I'll understand.'

I felt like running. A fire of hostility rose in me and it took all of my willpower to dampen it. Claire was still behind me and when I turned to look at her, I saw the wretched expression that I'd sometimes seen on the face of my mother when she was worried about something. I knew then that I'd stay.

Under my breath I said, 'It's okay, we're here now, we may as well stay. Don't worry, it'll be all right.'

Alice and Barb had reached the table and the waiter didn't look too happy about all the shuffling and bumping of chairs going on but Michael and his friends seemed very pleased to make room for us. They'd only arrived a few minutes before. Hadn't yet ordered their food.

I laughed at their attempt of an Australian greeting; it sounded like 'G'die.' Everyone in the group knew each other and Claire introduced me. We settled around the table above the 'hello' and 'how are you' of the others. With the camaraderie going on, I hardly noticed the moment of contact with Michael's hand, but I hesitated for an instant when the waiter seated me beside him.

By the time I'd fumbled around to find a spot at my feet for my bag, the group was chatting away to each other and the moment of awkwardness passed.

We had a confab about wine.

John: 'Have you tried…?' He didn't get time to finish.

Claire: 'Seeing as Anna comes from one of the world's best known wine states, I think she should choose.'

Michael: 'You been reading up on things Australian, Claire?'

Claire: 'Only the wine regions 'cos I like the product.'

Michael said nothing.

It was decided, because we were all eating fish of some kind, we'd start with a couple of bottles of Hardy's Rhine Reisling from the Barossa Valley. Once we'd settled on our choice from the menu and placed orders, a rush of questions about what I did in Australia had me turning my head to different faces around me. I felt like I was spotting all points on a compass. I told them a little bit about my studies and the frantic weeks of last semester.

I was fascinated by their accents. Their voices sounded deep and rich as if smothered in golden syrup. None of them used vernacular words like 'tae' or 'frae' like Grandpa or Fiona.

'What d'you think of our beach here? How does it compare to Bondi?' John asked.

'I've never actually been to Bondi,' I said, 'but I live a few minutes away from a beach where I can walk for miles on sand without pebbles. During January and February I go early in the morning – it's too hot to go in the middle of the day.'

They asked other questions about what music I liked and what I'd be doing in London. I felt that I was under scrutiny, but in a kindly sort of way.

Michael looked different from when I'd seen him at Finn Maccool's. He was about the same height and build as his mates. His hair and colouring were similar to the man sitting beside him but I felt a presence about him that I couldn't quite figure out. Something about him made him stand out from the crowd.

When we'd settled down to eat Michael asked me, 'Anna, d'you know anything about teaching jobs in Australia?'

'I don't offhand,' I said, 'but I s'pose it would depend on what you mean by teaching. Is it primary, secondary, tertiary level? I know that most emerging teachers work on contracts. I know we have a dire shortage of good teachers. Have you tried searching the net?'

'No, but that's on my list of things to do. I've been teaching here for ten years and I'm wondering if that counts for anything in Australia.' He went on to ask me about the price of houses and cars, bank interest rates and rental accommodation.

I could see Claire sitting quietly, picking at her food and watching Michael and me talking. She'd hardly said a word since we sat down. When we'd finished the main course, I asked Barb if she'd swap places with me and moved beside Claire.

'I've been worried that you'd be uncomfortable in a certain person's company,' she whispered.

'No, it's okay.' I watched the faces around me and realised it was true. I began to feel at ease, like I was sharing fellowship with the housemates at Augie's.

Claire relaxed beside me and began to join in the banter. I saw messages flick across the table between her and Michael when their eyes met.

Images began to separate and unravel in my head – like the string Grandpa and I had been working on – and it dawned on me that the tension from Claire was not based on my thoughts about Michael or his father; it was about her own feelings for Michael.

I heard again in my head Claire's words from the other night and recognised that I couldn't judge Michael on the sins of his father. I appreciated also that my mother would never want me taking revenge. She had managed in her own way to put it all behind her. I wished that I could re-write my previous meeting with Claire.

At that instant, a load lifted from my heart and a wonderful sense of freedom poured into me. I looked at Claire and smiled and I knew that she understood. It seemed to me that the wine, the food, the conversation and the smell of the sea had conspired to bring me a measure of peace.

## 67

When I got back to Granpa's, I told him about watching the march. 'Why does the hatred still… I mean, surely that's the stuff of Northern Ireland?'

'Well, ye see, lass, the west o' Scotland is peopled mainly wi' the descendants o' the victims o' the Irish famine o' the 1840s an' they brought their bigotry wi' them. So oor culture here is as Irish as Paddy's pigs. The violence was generated by the Battle of the Boyne and welded in tae the hearts o' a minority that keep it alive year after year.'

He went on to tell me that some of the marchers had been caught urinating on the steps of St Conval's and that they'd stopped outside the Catholic McSweeneys' house battering the big drum. Eddie McSweeney and two of his sons started waving green and gold flags from every window. The drum got louder and the flag-wavers lost their tempers and charged out to confront their foes. All hell broke loose and six of them ended up in jail with black eyes and broken noses.

'The drum was muffled for the time being and Mrs McSweeney hid the Catholic banners. But that's only till next year.'

'How do you cope with the noise?'

'Keep the blinds shut an' stay inside till they pass. It's a' I can dae. Cissie here gets agitated and cries a lot so I dae what I can tae keep her calm. We used tae go tae Kate's place at Oban at this time o' year but that ended when Cissie had the stroke.'

Until meeting Grandpa, old people had never interested me. I connected them to the smell of lavender and complaints about the government. Just about every sentence of old Mrs Daly's began 'In my day…' But being with Grandpa changed my opinion. His kindness to Grandma, his ability to mix and connect with Claire and her friends and his interest in history made for a surprising companionship.

What I learned through watching the people I met through my ears and eyes was a finer quality than any information garnered by sophisticated research.

170

## 68

On my last evening, Grandma was in her bedroom and I sat in the living room with Grandpa. I asked him what he'd done for a living.

'Och well, I spent my working life weaving carpets for Stoddart's. Of course they shut down in 1992 but I'd retired long afore that. Y'see that rug under your feet? Well, I was probably the man that watched bits o' wool transform intae that pattern. I tell ye, Anna, we were hard manual workers in they days. Have ye noticed how I cup my ear in my hand to help me hear better what folk are sayin?'

I nodded.

'Well, that's a legacy frae workin' inside a noisy loom for years.'

'You worked inside a machine?'

He gazed into space and for the next few minutes re-lived his days as a craftsman. I learned about stillages, dye lots and setting patterns. By the time he finished talking, I felt that I could weave a carpet myself.

'So what shape has your life taken since you retired?'

'Oh, I've been busy. What wi' the garden an' takin' wee trips up around the Highlands, I've hardly had time tae fill my pipe. Then of course the bowling has been a great social outlet – gi'es me a chance for a good natter wi' other retired pals. Since Cissie got sick of course, that's took up a lot o' my time an' energy.'

I then asked if he knew what had happened to Frank Welsh.

'Sure I know. He stays just doon the road that goes oot tae the new housin' scheme. Sometimes he can be seen wanderin' aroun' the streets.'

'Did the people of the village know that he raped Mum?'

Grandpa closed his eyes. Clenched his fists. Pursed his lips tight as if he was holding in a scream of terror. I wished I hadn't asked the question.

I didn't know what Frank Welsh looked like, but thought maybe I'd have sensed malevolence near me if I'd walked past him on one of my rambles through the village.

172

**69**

My thoughts scattered when I heard a thud and crash in the hallway and rushed to see what had happened.

Grandma stood waving her arm around at some albums lying on the floor. She'd been carting them to the lounge on the tray of her walker and they'd fallen off when her frame had collided with the door jamb.

She was saying something like 'F…tos, f…tos.'

Once I'd picked the books up, and we were settled down again, Grandpa said, 'This is somethin' we've treasured ower the years. I think your grandma wants you tae have them.'

The books were full of Mum's stories and artwork from her school days. Drawings of flowers and trees made with bright yellows, purples, greens and houses with red roofs, black brick chimneys and stick figures holding balls and skipping ropes. The stories started when she would've been about seven, the last one written on her twelfth birthday, a story about a young girl sailing on an ocean liner to America, getting shipwrecked and saved by a handsome deckhand.

One book was full of photos of Mum. Most of them were framed with ribbon or piping made from fabric that could have been parts of the dresses Mum was wearing in the snapshots. The pages were edged with pink and white lace. A photo of her in school uniform had a certificate beside it – an award for excellence in artwork. Another was framed within a silver bracelet that looked like it would've fitted around the wrist of a seven-year-old, the age she was in the photo. Neat handwriting beside each snap gave details about where and when the event had happened. Mum stood beside 'Eleanor's first dancing lesson 1951', in a ballet outfit with her hair held back from her face by a broad band. 'Eleanor's first day at school' was dated 1952.

The latest photo dated 1962 showed Mum beside another girl. They held bike handlebars with one hand while trying to keep their hair from flying away with the other. They were dressed in pedal pushers and T-shirts and they looked like they were sharing a joke of some kind.

'Who's that?' I asked Grandpa, pointing to the other girl.

'That's Fiona. Back then they were like Siamese twins, joined at the hip. I used tae love seein' them go off on their bikes. They were such a happy pair o' lassies.'

Fiona looked tiny and her smile was as wide as her face.

'Take these wi' you when you go,' Grandpa said, offering them to me with shaking hands.

I sensed that he wanted to give me something of my mother but at the same time, this was all he had of her and it would be hard for him to part with it.

'No, Grandpa, you keep them. I know she'd be pleased that you'd looked after them.'

'I'll share a wee secret wi' ye, Anna.' He lowered his voice and brought his head close to mine. 'The thing is, it was your grandma that put all this thegither. I had nothin' tae dae wi' it. Cissie spent months going through your mother's old school books an' packets o' photos we'd taken ower the years.

'In the evenin's when I watched TV or read the paper, she'd cut, glue, trim an' write. Sometimes I'd catch her cryin' and I'd make her a cup o' tea. S'funny, y'know, we never knew how tae talk aboot Ellie. We lost more than a daughter at that time. It took years before we found a way tae talk tae each ither. Ye see, Anna, Ellie never told us what had been done tae her or who had done it. I suspected, but your gran thought her refusal to marry Frank Welsh, was stubbornness – an' they were both sae strong-willed.'

Grandma came into my room while I was packing and sat on the bed. She started to make the same sound as before. 'Noa…uv…er' and again, 'Noa…uv…er.'

I sat beside her. 'Take your time,' I said.

She closed her eyes, squeezed them tight together, took a few deep even breaths, then, clear as a bell sound in a quiet room, she said, 'Eleanor, I loved her.'

We looked each other straight in the eye and laughed together. I stroked her back and she kissed my hands – both of them.

'I'm so impressed. In no time at all, you'll be speaking normally. Wish I'd more time to spend with you and we could have a real conversation.'

She held onto my hands and said again, 'Eleanor...I loved her... miss her,' and we both melted in tears.

It seemed to me that her words came from an understanding that my mother would never have thought possible. Whatever had happened in the past, I sensed Grandma's heartbreak and longing for the daughter she'd lost. I told her that I recognised this and that I could feel her pain. She nodded and, like she'd done the day we met, she let the tears roll down her face. I took a tissue from a box and soaked them up.

My parents were just as dead here as they'd been in Adelaide and no number of albums or talking about them could bring them back. Grandpa was cleaning his glasses when I said this to him just before I left.

'Anna,' he said, 'think about the years ye had wi' your mother, an' be grateful. That's what I dae when I miss her.'

It seemed to me then that the love my mother craved had jumped a generation and I was the beneficiary.

Fiona came over for a last cup of tea. 'It's like sayin' cheerio to your mam all over again, but wi' some luck we might get to see you again,' she said, wiping tears away.

I gave her my address and contact numbers and watched her walk along the path. She'd gone as far as the gate, and then she turned round and waved me towards her.

'You've forgotten something?' I asked.

'No,' Fiona said. 'I just want you to see somethin', or rather someone.' She pointed to an old man tottering along towards us.

He had a walking stick. His legs hardly able to hold him up. Thin white strands of hair were plastered to his head and the skin on his face had a bluish tinge around a bulbous nose. As he came closer, I could see frayed cuffs on a dirty shirt peeking out of tweed sleeves. The jacket he wore looked like it'd been lying in the mud somewhere. His trousers were wrinkled and showed a gap between the cuff and the top of his socks. He looked like one of the old derelicts I'd seen tottering along Rundle Mall with a long thin stick in one hand and plastic bags filled with empty drink containers in the other.

'Take a good look at that spectacle,' Fiona said and took hold of my arm.

'Why? Who is he?' I asked.

'Frank Welsh.'

I froze. Paralysed by the sight. Then I started shaking and tried to bolt back up the path.

Fiona held tight to me and whispered, 'Listen, Anna, can you see what I'm tryin' to tell you? This man is no' only friendless, he's hated and neglected. No' only because o' what he did to your mam, but he's made a lot o' people suffer in his life. Your mam was loved by many an' she had a good life in spite o' what he did.'

I stared at him. The hands that had probed and enjoyed my mother were now shaking with palsy. He mumbled under his breath as he passed us. I didn't know how old he would be now, but I figured he'd be at least thirty years younger than Grandpa. I watched his bent back totter to the end of the street.

Fiona hugged me again and crossed the oval with a last wave and a promise to keep in touch.

Alone in my room, I thought about Frank Welsh stalking the village streets wearing his own ugliness.

**70**

My mother's neglect of Fiona and the father she'd claimed to love had made me angry. But here in the room where she'd cried her youth away, I finally understood. By cutting all ties with the place where so much had happened to her, Mum had allowed herself the freedom she needed to build a beautiful life.

While I pressed jumpers and jeans into my suitcase I thought about Michael. I'd come close to hating him.

Claire arrived with Andy. 'Need someone to sit on your case?'

'Thanks, Claire, but it's almost shut. Guess who I saw a few minutes ago?'

'Mmmm, let me guess. Was it somebody old? Ugly?'

'Frank Welsh.'

'Thought it might have been. Just saw him at the end of the street. How did you know it was him?'

'Fiona was just leaving. She pointed him out to me.'

'Well now, Anna, that'll give you an idea of what Michael had to put up with.'

'I know. And I'm so very sorry for being angry with him. After all, the violence that changed Mum's life held him in Purgatory for a big slice of his. He doesn't deserve my venom to pollute his present.'

'Well, like I said to you earlier ,Anna, accept the truth of your mam's life and leave it in the past where it belongs.' Claire carried my suitcase out to the car and left me alone.

I wrote a thank you note and stuck it on a bottle of Scotch I'd bought for Grandpa. For Gran, I left a silk pale green dressing gown. I sat on the bed for a few minutes taking a last look around then hitched my backpack on and joined Claire.

I'd learned that I was capable of feeling a hatred I'd never known before. I accepted I'd no room in my heart for absolving a decrepit old man of his sin against my mother, but a corner of understanding for his son uncovered itself in my soul.

# 71

When I left that last morning, Grandma stood beside Grandpa holding onto the gate waving a white hankie. Grandpa looked forlorn standing by the kerbside with his Akubra hat tilted to the back of his head and his arms stretched out with an empty hug, waiting for someone to fill the space. I got in the car and didn't look back at them or at the gate where a clump of rosemary had crept around the hinges, but at the garden bench where a neat ball of twine sat in a corner. Then I think I held my eyes shut for a minute and when I opened them we were on the freeway heading to the airport.

Andy broke the silence. 'Maybe you'll get another trip to Scotland before ye head back to Australia.'

'Yes. Maybe. I'd like that.'

Too soon, and with mixed feelings, I said goodbye to Andy, Jack and Claire at Glasgow Airport. I hadn't seen Michael since the day we'd gone to Ayr. I asked Claire to give him a big hug for me.

She reached her arms out and said, 'Here's one from him.'

When I'd planned this trip, I'd thought that fitting into their lives would've been easy, like putting on a glove or a warm scarf or by simply getting on a plane and flying across boundaries. But my life didn't flow into their world. The echoes that had come to me through my mother were fainter here and grew fainter with each passing day. Things will stay as they were before I arrived here and forever I will see them like so many frames in still photos. I draped an 'invisible cloak of words of love' around them and left them as I'd found them.

**72**

Within a few hours of leaving Scotland I'd had my first taste of London's noisy, smelly congested streets, been registered into my course and took possession of the flat I'd arranged in the halls of residence.

The city clanged with the bedlam of shops, hotels, restaurants and people charging through their days. It seemed to me that London had a conviction that it was the sole reason all people existed. The only place I felt safe was in my room with my own things around me. Everything I needed was within walking distance from the lecture hall. The rooms were clean with access to reasonably good food. Staying at uni was the best option.

The skies of London looked like unpolished silver – just a shade lighter than the grey of the streets. I began to miss the brilliant blue expanse of Australia's high skies and the innocence of swimming alone in a sea surging to beaches miles long, and the freedom of shorts and flip-flops. Mostly, I missed the camaraderie of the house mates. I missed Joe.

Euston Station was three blocks away from my residence and during my wanderings of the first week, I envisaged my mother and Fiona walking these streets. I imagined them trying to look sophisticated and failing, because of their innocence.

As often as I could, I walked to the National Art Gallery and stood in front of the van Dyck painting showing a proud Charles I on his charger and thought of the violence of the times when this stubborn ruler had lived. And the years of civil war when Cromwell's soldiers had pillaged the churches, knocked down holy statues, then lit their pipes from candles on the altar and pissed from the pulpit. Sometimes, I'd spend the whole day in the British Museum or the university library researching the days of ordinary people of my study period. People like Samuel Pepys who, as a schoolboy, waited at Whitehall to see the execution of Charles I then, eleven years later, watched the triumphant return of Charles II when the bleak Cromwellian experiment had failed.

One day, an invitation to present a paper at the Fifth International Symposium on Milton's work appeared in my pigeonhole. On the day of the conference I woke early, read my notes and skimmed Book 1 of *Paradise Lost*.

I couldn't eat breakfast that morning. Nerves made my hands shake and my stomach felt like an embattled fortress of buzzing, flying lurching things I'd no name for. I strolled around Bread Street and Cheapside hoping that, in spite of modern restaurants, shops and theatres, this part of London would serve as a conduit to the spirit of Milton, and help me deliver his ideas with a touch of his poetic passion.

In the foyer of the meeting hall, I stood against a wall to the right of the entrance, eavesdropping on conversations, hoping to pick up some useful hints about other academic offerings, but the voices talked low and my ears wouldn't tune into the accents.

When I was introduced, I stepped up to the podium, took a few deep breaths and read with confidence. I finished speaking exactly on time, and as I gathered up my papers and shut down the projection system, strangers came up to me with questions and comments about the research I'd done. A group of women I'd seen near my flat invited me to lunch and we spent the afternoon swapping stories about London and Adelaide.

## 73

I'd emailed Mardi a few times to ask how she was getting on without me. She usually replied within a couple of days but I hadn't heard from her in weeks. Finally, she wrote, 'I'm in Kuala Lumpur. Meet me by the lions in Trafalgar Square on Sunday around two.'

Trust Mardi. Never gives a person a chance to respond. By three o'clock on Sunday, she hadn't arrived and I was thinking I'd got the date wrong.

I was about to walk across to the National Gallery when I heard 'Anna! Anna! Over here! Look up!' She was waving her red scarf madly from the open top of a tourist bus. Someone sitting beside her was laughing. I watched both of them scramble for the exit and made my way to the nearest bus stop. Mardi and I danced around on the pavement and laughed and hugged each other.

The person, who'd been beside her on the bus, waited and watched our performance, then he said, 'You don't recognise me. Think I'll catch the next plane back to Adelaide.'

I heard the voice and looked at the eyes. 'Joe! I can't believe it! What've you done? Where's your beard, your fuzzy hair? Your beanie?'

'It's great to see you too, Anna,' he said, laughing and reaching out his arms to me. It was lovely to catch his particular smell as if he'd brought Australia with him.

'That's the first time I've heard you say a complete sentence without the F word. You got religion or something?'

'Nah, thought I'd let you hear the real me.'

'I'm so glad you came. All we need now is Augie!'

'Augie's meditating somewhere in India, then he's off to the States and I've quit my job back home,' Mardi said. 'I can stay overseas as long as I want to. Now let's get to one of those archaic drinking holes.'

Joe wore a trendy jacket. A Tommy Hilfiger shirt with a collar had replaced his old jumper. His jeans and boots were spotless and his hair was styled like a sixties schoolboy. He looked like he'd blend into a weekend gathering of business people. We linked arms and headed to the Font and Firkin.

'What about you, Joe?' I asked, sipping on warm beer.

'Contract with Hull University until Christmas. Start in three weeks. Fuckin' office work.'

'Looking forward to it?'

'Maybe. Don't know yet. Depends.'

'On what?'

Joe's clean-shaven face had suddenly gone red.

Mardi said, 'See you in a minute.' and bustled off to the ladies.

'I wanna ask you something,' he said stroking his chin as if he was searching for the beard that had hid his shyness.

'Ask anything. What's on your mind?'

'I've missed you a lot, and I'd like you and I to spend time together just the two of us. I'd like you to get to know how I feel about you. I promise to watch my language and dress right.'

'Joe, you're fine the way you are. I wouldn't want you to change for me.'

He gave one of his lopsided, innocent smiles. 'Here,' he said, handing me a package rough-wrapped in cellophane. It was a box with pictures of koalas nestled in gum trees. Inside, it held a soft white dog with brown ears that looked like the frizzy ringlets Joe used to have. The dog had a gum leaf tucked behind each ear.

'Name's Milton,' he said, and studied my face.

'Thank you, Joe. I love it. Great name.'

74

The three of us explored London for the next few days. Then Mardi left for the ancient pubs of Europe with a promise to come back to London when she stopped having a good time.

After she'd gone and until Joe had to start work, he met me at the end of each uni day and we'd go to some restaurant that he'd found during his day's wanderings.

We took a train trip to Windsor, where we stood outside the house of Christopher Wren, then watched the sons of aristocrats saunter around Eton College. We inspected memorials of kings and poets in Westminster Abbey. I read on Dylan Thomas's tombstone, 'Time held me green and dying though I sang in my chains like the sea.'

One day we took a trip to Hampton Court Palace.

'Can you feel the history in these cobblestones?' I asked Joe as we walked about.

'No history here. These've been laid…let me think…about five years ago.'

'How d'you know that?'

'S'easy – see that bronze plaque?' He pointed to a spot about two metres away. 'It's got a redevelopment date on it.' He hooted with laughter and grabbed my threatening umbrella. Then he held me close while people around us laughed at our happiness.

That night, Joe moved into my flat. At times during those first days, I floated outside my body. Needing nothing. Being. It was a feeling of comfort; of being safe with a person, not having to weigh or measure words; just pouring them all out, like pouring tea full of flavour. It felt wonderful to have this large and gentle man by my side.

Some mornings we'd lie late and make a Gregorian chant out of our names. 'Joe…An…Na, An…Na…Joe,' we'd sing it to each other, then laugh remembering Augie and his yogic mantras.

Then Joe would whisper, 'Nothing…else…is.'

# 75

During the next weeks, each time I looked in the mirror, I was surprised to see the same face looking back at me.

By November the foggy greyness of winter in London had seeped into my bones. Joe had settled into his job in Hull and we grabbed weekends of love and wonder together until my time in England was up.

My course at uni finished before Joe's contract and we agreed that the sensible thing to do was for me to go back to Adelaide and wait for him.

I don't remember when I first realised that I'd fallen in love with Joe but I think having an arm or leg amputated would've been less painful than the feeling I had when we parted at Heathrow.

I felt bereft without his hands holding mine and wanted him beside me on the plane. We'd be separated for a few weeks and worries about terrorist attacks and plane crashes left me desperate with fear for him and for us.

The smells of eucalyptus, the warmth of sun rays and the smoothness of sandy beaches stretched all the way across oceans and mountains, through London's clutter to clutch at my heart. Adelaide pulled me back to wide high skies and sunshine and a life with Joe.

# Heathrow Departure Lounge

Still fifty minutes till boarding. I'm Fidgeting. Pacing. Checking passport and Customs papers. Sit. Stand. Walk. Spying a computer terminal on the far wall of the lounge becoming available I grabbed the opportunity to check my email.

Emails between Claire and me had kept each of us up to date. She'd ask how I was doing in London and tell me things about her social life and how Grandma and Grandpa were getting along. I'd promised to let her know when I arrived safely home and didn't expect to hear from her again until then, but her name was first on the In Box list.

She wrote,

Hi Anna,

Guess what? I'm coming to Australia. Not only me. Michael's coming too (long story – will fill you in later). Can you believe that? We'll arrive before Christmas. Date/time later.

We've both got jobs lined up. Before I start searching the net for accommodation in Adelaide, we were wondering if we could stay with you for a week or so until we get our bearings. We'd really appreciate that.

Love from Claire (and Michael too). Xx

It took about a minute to email her back and let her know I was okay with Michael and that I'd love to have them. The thought of being in my own home with real family and someone special in my life warmed the very core of my heart.

When the plane finally descended over the browning hills of my corner of the world, I watched the sea swamp the beaches and pictured Joe and me walking along with our shoes in our hands and summer cottons clinging to our bodies. He'd fling me into the sea and we'd laugh like children. Later we'd lie on the sand, eat pizza and sing our own songs to each other.

I thought about Claire and me shopping in Adelaide and sharing times and events in our lives. I wondered if one day Fiona would come to Adelaide and we'd sit at my kitchen table drinking pots of tea and she'd keep me amused with her stories.

I thought about Mum and her writings snuggled amongst my things. And I thought too that the worst thing about my mother dying was that she'd never know about the pictures of her life that had been so cherished over the years.

Like a river turning back on itself, my journey would end where it began.

# Acknowledgements

While writing this fictional story, I consulted numerous articles regarding the Polaris submarine base in the Holy Loch in 1960s Scotland. The article on page 50 is a fiction based on information at http://www.history.navy.mil/danfs/h9/hunley.htm on 24/04/2004.

Maps of London and the town of Oban helped me place my characters geographically.

The poem 'Beannacht' is from *Anam Cara: Spiritual Wisdom from the Celtic World* by John O'Donohue, published by Bantam Press, reprinted by permission of the Random House Group Ltd.

The title *I Dream of Magda* is used with kind permission of the author, Stefan Laszczuk.

The quote from Yeats appears in 'When You Are Old', reproduced in full overleaf.

At the time of writing, I was fortunate to have my mother close by. I give thanks that she had the ability to recall copious tales about the American 'invasion'. Her anecdotal evidence, and her repertoire of ancient Scottish/Irish songs were priceless.

Thank you to the Creative Writing Department of the University of Adelaide, especially to my supervisor Jan Harrow and my tutorial friends Alice Sladden, Ian Bone and Stefan Laszczuk for their invaluable input and encouragement.

Encouragement came in cartloads from the South Australian Writers Centre. Thank you to Barbara Wiesner, Jude Aquilina and Malcolm Walker for your legendary support.

To Stephen Matthews and Brenda Eldridge at Ginninderra Press, thank you for recognising the 'soul' in my story, and for your patience.

Thank you, always and ever, to Anne Marie for sharing the burden.

Your constancy and loyalty are the expressions of your beautiful character. Big hug to Courtney for reminding me about what is really important in life.

To the men in my life: Paul who has walked the rocky road with me and kept me centred; Dale, my ever-constant techo, without you, I'd still be in the dark ages of pen and ink; Leigh, you are an inspiration on how to cope with the 'slings and arrows' life throws at us; Bryce, thank you for being there when my 'to do' list appears daunting; Mackenzie, for helping with the practicalities of life and for brightening my place with your happy face.

Special thanks to my friends Henry Ashley-Brown and Stephanie Thomson for another year of literary support, discussions and friendship. The seeds of many stories have been planted.

To my walking group friends Sue, Val, Mariann and Pam: we walk and we talk and we eat our way through subjects eternal and relevant to life's big issues. Thank you.

To my siblings: thank you for helping me through the dark times. Now we are eight, but still… 'Here's tae us, wha's like us.'

# When You Are Old

When you are old and grey and full of sleep,
And nodding by the fire, take down this book,
And slowly read, and dream of the soft look
Your eyes had once, and of their shadows deep:

How many loved your moments of glad grace,
And loved your beauty with love false or true,
But one man loved the pilgrim soul in you,
And loved the sorrows of your changing face:

And bending down beside the glowing bars,
Murmur, a little sadly, how Love fled
And paced upon the mountains overhead
And hid his face amid a crowd of stars.